# THE INTIMATE ONES

# THE INTIMATE ONES

## BONNIE GOLIGHTLY

*Includes a rare author profile and interview*

# Bonnie Golightly:
## Author Still Living in the Shadow of Her Name
By Wendi Watts

*Editor's note: This rare profile of Bonnie Golightly includes an extensive interview conducted shortly before her death. The article is reprinted with permission from the Lifestyles section of* The Daily News Journal *of Murfreesboro, Tennessee, Sunday, August 30, 1998, © Wendi Watts — USA TODAY NETWORK via Imagn Images.*

Bonnie Golightly might have remained an enigma of Murfreesboro's past, but for a conversation at The Woman's Club last winter that set the memories of her in motion again.

While chatting at a December meeting of The Woman's Club, a member who had not grown up here commented on the number of literary connections in the community…Charles Egbert Craddock [pen name of Mary Noailles Murfree], Andrew Nelson Lytle, Andre Norton, Will Allen Dromgoole…

And a native of the city asked, "Have you heard of Truman Capote?"

"Yes, but what's the connection to Murfreesboro?" the newcomer naively asked.

*'That Capote Thing'*

The main character in Capote's short book "Breakfast at Tiffany's," which was turned into a movie starring Audrey Hepburn, may have been modeled on a woman who grew up in Murfreesboro.

The character, Holly Golightly, bears some striking similarities to the real woman, Bonnie Golightly.

The daughter of an MTSU professor of education, Bonnie grew up in the shadow of the university's campus from the mid-1920s to the mid-'40s. She went to dances and parties and was regularly mentioned in *The Daily News Journal*'s Partyline column.

Until recently, most of "the crowd" who used to hang out at the Golightly house at 1212 East Main St.—Susan Bragg, Kacky Holden, Charlotte Dill, Frances Nelson—thought Bonnie was dead. Others weren't sure. A few thought she was probably alive somewhere living as only Bonnie could.

To later generations, tales of her youth in Murfreesboro and later life in New York have been regarded as containing a grain of truth and a large measure folklore.

But Bonnie is very real and very much alive.

And she may forever be defined and, much to her chagrin, remembered mostly by one event that brought her national attention—what she refers to as "that Capote thing."

During World War II, Bonnie and her husband, Bob Sheffield, moved to Greenwich Village, where Bonnie owned and operated a bookstore called The Park Book Shop. She later divorced Sheffield but continued living and working in the city.

At the same time, Truman Capote was living in New York and making a name for himself as a writer. Among his most famous works set in that era is the novella *Breakfast at Tiffany's*.

Holly Golightly was the story's main character, a charming 19-year-old cat lover with an aversion to attachments of any kind—a wild thing not meant to be held down by social conventions.

Holly's fictional life and Bonnie's real one shared many similarities—growing up in the South, living in a brownstone on Manhattan's East Side with a bar around the corner on Lexington, singing folk music, having an assortment of dramatic and theatrical friends and acquaintances and having a love of cats.

"I knew an awful lot of people who knew Capote," Bonnie said in a recent telephone interview from her home in New Haven, Conn. "I did not know Capote at all, and he denied all of his life that he had based the book on me. After he died…somebody admitted in *New York Magazine* that he had based the whole thing on me."

Capote "knew somebody who knew me very well, a bitch, who really bitched the hell out of me," the 79-year-old recalled. "She was somebody who, she thought she had taken away my boyfriend. My boyfriend returned to me and she really had it in for me from then on. And I got backlash for years, *years*. She apparently talked to Capote and Capote didn't know I still lived in New York or anything else, and he thought he was perfectly safe in using my name.

"I first heard about this from a friend, David Lubis, also a writer—a published writer—who lived in an apartment I had lived in a few months before.

"Christmastime came and I dropped by the apartment to see if I'd gotten any mail and he said, 'Oh, I didn't know you existed!' And I said, 'What do you mean?' And he told me he had heard Capote read from a work in progress…and the name [of the main character] had been Connie Golightly. 'Connie,' for constantly traveling.

"And so I said, 'I'm not going to put up with this,' and called up Hiram Haydn…somebody I knew at Random House [publishing company], and said, 'Please don't let Capote use my name.'"

Bonnie was told the name "Golightly" had been used before in literature and was not unheard of as the name of a character.

"But…from what I had been told about the work in progress, there were too many similar things," Bonnie explained. "I just didn't want it. And I especially didn't want it because I was a writer myself and I didn't want him to use my name.

"So Hiram went to Capote, who agreed to change the name, and the name was changed to 'Holly Golightly,'" Bonnie said, and added with more than a tinge of sarcasm in her voice, "Big deal."

*Breakfast at Tiffany's* was published by Random House in 1958 and appeared in *Esquire* magazine the same year.

Bonnie was so outraged, she filed libel and invasion of privacy lawsuits asking for $800,000 against Capote, *Esquire* and Random House, according to an article in *Time* magazine.

The *Time* article appeared in the Feb. 9, 1959, issue and said, Capote "claims that his Holly had three 'counterparts in reality,' none of them Bonnie. 'One of them is dead—she died in Africa, the other two are very much alive and have no intention of suing me.'"

Capote also is quoted in response to Bonnie's lawsuit as saying, "I have never met nor seen this lady.… It's ridiculous for her to claim she is my Holly."

Capote never publicly revealed whom he based the character of Holly Golightly on, but a number of women who knew the author have seen themselves in her. Author Doris Lilly, novelist Pati Hill, artist Beatrice Whistler [Dabney] and actress Carol Grace all claim to have been his inspiration, according to information posted on an Internet site about *Breakfast at Tiffany's*.

But Bonnie claims she paid a high price for Capote's work because she shared her last name with his character.

"It really semi-ruined my writing life," Bonnie says. "I'm not kidding you.… I was advised by publishers to change my name. I had become a figment of [Capote's] imagination.… It was very discouraging, first of all. It made me feel as if I were a bird that had its wings pulled off.… Afterward, I didn't write very much on my own. I wrote mostly things that editors would come to me and ask me to write for them."

Bonnie's lawyer dropped the lawsuit.

The Capote incident is still a thorn in Bonnie's side, and she continues to fight to have her writing and contributions to the body of American literature recognized, contributions her friends from childhood had no doubt Bonnie would make.

*Memories of Murfreesboro*

Born June 23, 1919, in Chicago to Thomas J. and Emily Rogers Golightly, Bonnie was their second child. Her brother, Thomas Jr., was seven years older.

When Bonnie was an infant, the family moved to North Dakota.

In 1925, the family moved to Murfreesboro, where her father joined the faculty at Middle Tennessee Normal College. Bonnie began her formal education at Campus School in what is now known as Kirksey Old Main on the MTSU campus.

Among her first-grade classmates was Susan Lytle, now the wife of John Bragg, retired state representative.

"I knew her all the way through school," Susan recalled. "She wrote quite a bit. I can remember her sitting in class and not paying a bit of attention because she was writing short stories. And she was good…. Even in grade school, she came and did what she wanted. I guess that's what made her different.

"She was very independent. She had a good mind, but she didn't care about school at all," Susan continued. "I can still see her in English class with a tablet just writing up a storm…. She had no discipline. If she liked you, she was a friend. She could tell you off if she wanted to."

Even as a child, Bonnie knew she wanted to be a writer.

"Everybody in my family wrote," she recalled. "I started writing when I was 8 years old. I wrote stories…things about playmates. You know, silly little things."

After completing grammar school at Campus, Bonnie attended Central High School.

During these years, the Golightly home was the regular meeting place for Bonnie's friends and acquaintances.

"I had an awful lot of friends in Murfreesboro," Bonnie said. "We had a 'crowd' as we called it. There were about 10 of us in the crowd. Susan was one of them. Emily Crichlow, Juanita Highman… We'd meet after school, largely, and then at night, too, on weekends. We always had parties on weekends, very often at my house…. I don't know why it was…. I had my own car when I was 14, a Willys-Knight roadster with a rumble seat, apple green. Very cute car."

One of the reasons the Golightly house was such a popular spot was that Bonnie's parents were more permissive than most in Murfreesboro at that time, members of the crowd explained.

"The [Golightly] household was not quite run like anyone else's in Murfreesboro," Susan said. "There were no restrictions."

"The gang seemed to go to her house on Friday nights," recalled Charlotte Dill, another member of the crowd. "I guess we liked to go there because Bonnie wouldn't let her mother and daddy bother us."

But all of Bonnie's memories of growing up in Murfreesboro are not happy.

"They used to say that it had 10,000 people," Bonnie said.

"Actually, there were 7,900. Everybody knew everybody. I mean, there were people one simply did not know. You knew their names; that was it. It was a very snobby place. It was just awfully snobby. When the Cotillion Club was formed, a lot of really nice people got blackballed for no good reason. Meanness.

"My parents were older than my friends' parents, so my parents did not socialize with my friends' parents, so it made sort of a gap. But I was never top drawer really. I was secret top drawer…. It was a complicated thing."

Bonnie did not want to stay in Murfreesboro. She didn't know where she wanted to go, but she did know what she wanted to do.

Since she was a child, Bonnie longed to be a writer.

"Our house was right on the edge of town in those days," Bonnie said. "The city limits were about a half mile away from 1212 E. Main St. And I used to sit on the front steps and think, 'I really don't want to go North, but look at all those interesting cars going by…. I really don't want to stay here, but I don't want to go North."

*Experiences in Literature*

North, though, is where she ended up when she married Bob Sheffield, one of her father's students at the university. Bob had grown up in New York and Connecticut.

The couple moved to New York, where Bonnie opened and operated Park Book Shop from 1943-48. The shop specialized in out-of-print and rare editions.

From 1949-53, she was assistant manager at Hacker Art Books at Hacker Art Gallery.

Since 1954, she has been a freelance writer and editor, currently working as an editor with *Writer's Digest*.

"I knew an awful lot of people, but I didn't know them well," she explained. "I'm one of those people who can name drop and name roll, but that's about it. I didn't have close associations with most of them…. [Poet and author] William Carlos Williams was the only one I knew very, very well in that group. I met an awful lot of his friends too. But I knew him quite well.

"He was living in Rutherford, N.J., at the time. But he came into New York frequently as people do in New Jersey and Connecticut. They come into the city for one reason or another. And I met him because I had read something called *In the Money*. He wrote three novels, and that's one of them. And I wrote him a fan letter. He came by the shop and was fascinated. So, we became friends, and he and Josie, his wife, invited me to their house by the bay, and I would go out there frequently. And William game me copies of all his books.

Bonnie became an author in her own right. She has penned 20 books, including novels, mysteries, gothic fantasies and romances. She also did novelizations of movies such as *Legend of the Lost*, *The High Cost of Loving*, and *Olympia* for Avon book publishers.

During her writing career, she has used the pen names Milton Rogers, her maternal grandfather's name, and Helen Sheffield.

Her most successful books have been *Shades of Evil*, a

mystery, and *The Wild One*, a novel about an upper-class teenager who falls in and out of love with an older man.

Her first novel was based on a memory of Murfreesboro.

"The first novel I wrote was about…an incident down in the bottoms [in Murfreesboro]." Bonnie said. "I don't know if you still call it the bottoms or not, near the river. Poor people lived there.

"And there was a little boy who had a wolf on a chain, and I saw this wolf. We used to drive around all the time. It's one of the things we'd do…and I'd see this wolf on this chain and that was the basis of my first novel, which nearly got published."

Her favorite work is the last one published, titled *Polly Paris*, a gothic tale now out of print.

"I wrote eight books before I ever got published," Bonnie said. "I didn't get published until the early '50s. And I never would have gotten published, I suppose, except for having connections. That's the only way you really get ahead in this damn business…. I had a friend who worked for Avon books, and she commissioned the first book."

Among the books she wrote for Avon are *Beat Girl*, *The Intimate Ones* and *The Integration of Maybelle Brown*.

The last book she wrote, *The Veil of Order*, was about memories of Murfreesboro. It remains unpublished.

"I wrote that for myself," Bonnie said. "It nearly got published countless times. And it got to the point an editor would call and say, 'Let's have lunch,' and I'd say, 'Are you going to publish my book?' They'd say, 'Let's talk about it.' And I'd say, 'No thank you,' because at least 20 times that happened."

The 1,200-page book "was about Murfreesboro and made-up stuff about the South…. It's really not about Murfreesboro per se. There was nobody in it identifiable. But it was an amalgam. It was a saga opening in the late 19th century and went up to 1946, I think, something like that. There were similarities to people I knew."

Bonnie produces her work on a typewriter and never revises.

"I sit down and I write until I drop," Bonnie explained. "The longest I think I ever wrote without really stopping except to get up and answer the phone or open a can of soup was 125 pages."

That was a 12-hour write-a-thon.

She has the plots for her stories in her head.

"And then, the voices talk to me and tell me what to say, I've always said," Bonnie said. "It's a ridiculous kind of way to characterize it, but that's pretty much the truth…. But I simply cannot revise. I have tried, and I ruin it every time I try."

When inspiration strikes, she usually starts writing immediately.

"If I get interrupted, it's usually forever," Bonnie said. "The long book, *The Veil of Order*, I got interrupted and it took me, I think, a couple of years before I finally finished it. It just died on the vine."

She added that writers have their own preferences in how they create their work.

"Writing is such an individual thing that you can hardly characterize that it should be this way or that way or the other way," she said. "It's whatever way it comes out. That's the best advice to give any writer."

Her days now are filled with reading, writing and taking care of the six cats who share her home in New Haven—three inside, three out.

What does she plan to write in the future?

"I don't know," Bonnie replied. "I guess, I just…thought I had something to say, and one of the reasons I don't write much anymore is that I don't have anything to say."

*

Maybe so.

But her old chums at Murfreesboro's Woman's Club, where Bonnie's mother was once a member, have plenty to say about their friendships with Bonnie Golightly. And they are certain the book will never close on their memories of the wild young girl who will always live in the shadow of her name.

# THE INTIMATE ONES

*For Ben Gollay*

.

I

Stephen ogled the every-inch-a-lady in the sable jacket as she checked out of the hotel and frankly asked himself which he wanted more: a good hot bath or a good hot lay, but the question was purely academic at the moment, there being time for neither, and he clamped his mind shut on the subject as if it were a steel trap, and got on with his business.

It was his turn at the desk and the clerk said, "No mail, Mr. Marvell, I'm afraid, no telegrams either," with just that note of professional apology which made it seem not only his personal regret, but somehow his personal fault. And Stephen McCoy, alias Andrew Marvell, who would have been astounded to receive either form of communication had the truth been known, gave the clerk a nod of forgiveness and strolled to the elevator, idly swinging his key to room number 607.

In the elevator, Stephen received the same respectful nod from the operator which he had been accorded for the last five days: the nod of the lackey to the gentleman. And Stephen McCoy regretted, as he was borne upward to floor six without having to ask for it, that it was impossible to lengthen the life span of Andrew Marvell. Andrew Marvell, alias Stephen McCoy, had enjoyed his stay, for it was a very good hotel indeed. Just to his tastes: small, exclusive, quiet; tucked away on a street of the same quality and size. But the time had come when Andrew Marvell, as Mark Proost, S.T. Elliott, Thomas Traherne, Jr., and some half dozen other illustriously literary pseudonymed Stephen McCoys before him, must cease to be.

At his floor, Stephen gave the deferent elevator man a smile so faint that it was more telepathic than. muscular, and stepped out into the thickly carpeted hall. It was a good smile. It held geniality, yet restraint—a gentleman's smile. Carefully copied from the real thing observed in other hotel elevators. It was a smile which Stephen would dearly love to own. The rich and well born had it all over the working clowns, No more of that "we the people" stuff for him. Let the people have the people; they deserved them.

Almost angrily, he twisted the key in the lock and entered his foyer. He switched on the light, threw his chesterfield on the large comfortable chair—$500 bucks, at the very least, even at wholesale—and went over to the color TV set which he turned on rather absently. After that, he went around switching on all the lamps, so that the cheerful, expensive room was a radiant blur of soft, tasteful color, joined shortly by the vivid blaze of the TV program which was a almost harsh and out of keeping with the rest. But he liked it that way; he liked lots of light (especially if he didn't pay the bill) and a touch of the vulgar. Subtlety was greatly overrated: in art, literature, life. If something were truly alive, it was alive all the way, like a hot woman.

With this thought, he consulted his new wristwatch; a gift, as a matter of fact, from one of the best watchmakers in the world— a subtle gift, one they didn't know they had made. Which was an example of the perfect blend between the subtle and the vulgar: it was vulgar to steal, but subtle to do it expertly. But where in the hell were those women? He didn't look at his watch again; he didn't need to. They were just late. Late, as usual, the hot one and the lukewarm one. The latter, who was inclined to be whiney and who always asked "Why?" would never understand about punctuality. It wasn't enough for her that he said so, that was why. True, punctuality in this particular operation, had only a relative value, but it was a good habit, the habit of leaders. Great men seldom overslept.

He paced and he scowled, his stride resolute and brisk, more tycoon than military, and he darted little licks of fury in the direction of the silent telephone as if his large obsidian-hard black eyes were miniature flame throwers. Gradually his pacing became slower, and his eye took on a thoughtful look.

He sat down in still another easy chair, not far from the phone, and for a moment remained absolutely motionless with thought. Then he broke his absorption, and, with a sigh, reached in his pocket and pulled out the hotel bill given him that morning. To pass the time, he perused it, idly totaling up the various extra charges beside the exorbitant room charge and the tax: the local telephone calls, room service twice, and an item for dry cleaning that seemed much out of line. All in all, he marveled at the size of it, and wondered where on earth people got so much money these days. He discarded the bill suddenly, stood up and went to the closet to check his luggage again.

It was all packed, and neatly, as was his way, consisting of two newish suitcases. He looked at them fondly. They had been very expensive, though of course he hadn't actually bought them. He had gotten them on an exchange. They were of leather, light in weight and color, suitable for a man or a woman—exactly the kind seen in any first-class luggage store, on any first-class air flight, in every first-rate hotel. They were conservative, refined and totally unimaginative. Chosen for that reason.

Leaving his suitcases as if they were two friends, he went to the pantry bar and poured himself the last of the Scotch to which he added one cube of ice. He swished the liquid around in the glass for a while, as if this were a private process for cooling it and exclusively his, then he drank it in one large swallow, and put the glass down, completely satisfied: with self and drink. With that he readdressed his attention to the phone, his face hardening like that of a stem parent looking at a willful child.

Obediently, it rang.

His voice, as he answered, was cool, composed, and faintly rich, as if it were not a voice at all, but the merest suggestion of a very costly men's cologne.

The woman's voice on the other end was a little hoarse, slightly coarse, but affected and immature. "Darling," it said, "We're taking the 8:02."

He frowned. "The 8:02? Why not the 6:10? I was sure you could get a reservation on it."

"No," the woman corrected him swiftly. "Apparently it was all full up. We tried for something—uh—around seven, as we thought it would be more convenient, but the 8:02 was all we could get."

He was silent a moment, continuing to frown. "Well, as long as you don't miss connection."

"I'm sure we won't," the woman said cheerfully and gave a small laugh. Will we meet at the center staircase?"

"No, no," he said hastily. "The one on the left."

"All right, Uncle Andy!" The gay, and slightly vulgar voice came again, and he hung up without bothering to tell her good-bye. There was no need, for he would be seeing her in thirty minutes.

## II

That was the way they always worked it, or had since they had been working it at all. For the last few months, since the three of them, he and Gloria (the hot one. She should be since it was not only her oldest profession, but her primary one—) and Ellen (the lukewarm one. And no wonder, since she came from that nice Southern churchgoing background) had come from Chicago to New York, via the thumb, on the spur of the moment, they had worked the hotel trick this way. With few variations, barring slip-ups. And there had been only one or two of those, and so far, no close calls.

Tonight was a pushover night, despite the fact that Ellen and Gloria had not been able to check into room 610, as he had hoped when the occupant had checked out that morning. As Gloria had said, it was already reserved. Such slight misfortunes one must allow for.

As he rapidly walked up and down his room waiting for thirty minutes to pass, he pondered the next day's operations. While the girls spent the day in the stores he would settle down in his next hotel room and get some work done, for though he could not use a typewriter (carrying such a distinctive piece of luggage about was too risky) he had such a fierce drive to get this thing on paper that he was really quite happy to be doing it longhand. In another two weeks, as he figured it, it would be finished, then he would simply use the Redbook, locate some typing service, get it dashed off, neatly and probably more professionally than he could, even with his exacting standards. Then off to the publishers'—he had a list of the top ones systematically lined up—then they would see. They could all three quit this racket then if they wanted to. Or maybe just two of them. To hell with this threesome; he was tired of it. Or maybe he was just tired of it altogether, though it had been good. Maybe it was better to cut them loose and start out fresh on his own. Maybe...

He was quite excited thinking about it. This, in addition to the excitement he always felt when Andrew Marvell or Mark Proost or Mr. Giotto (for after all he had often been taken for an Eye-tie instead of a Mick) was about to "check out." It gave him a feeling of rich, historic satisfaction to be able to resurrect these names, even as a joke. Only once had the joke seemed reckless: when a clerk had scratched his head thoughtfully and said with a slight suspicion: "Dillon Thomass. That name is certainly familiar," then before Stephen could ease his mind, he broke into a glad wreath of smiles, as pathetic as paper flowers, snaped his fingers and said, "Danny Thomas. Of course!"

"Of course," Stephen had jovially agreed and continued to sign the registry, feeling sharper than ever. And one day, quite soon now, the name of Stephen McCoy would be as literarily elite as the others. For he was sure of this book. The others, admittedly, had not been right. But this one had, as so many advised, been entirely written "from his own experience." He yearned, this instant, to be settled into the new hotel, and writing. He glanced at his watch. Those cows had better be on time. But he could count on Gloria; at least she had never let him down at this stage. Two minutes to go.

Quickly, now, he went to the closet and picked up his suit-cases. He left them just inside the door and stepped carefully into the hall. He looked up and down. No one. Then he went to the stair door, carefully opened it and looked up. They were waiting.

He nodded to them, and they followed him down, the slight, almost too-pale blonde, and the taller girl with red hair and the voluptuous figure.

Keeping a little behind him, silently, they walked down the hall to room 607. He opened the door and each immediately took up a suitcase, and without a word the two girls left him and went back the way they bad come, bearing his luggage to their room.

After he had seen the stair door noiselessly being closed, he went inside 607, gave a fleeting look around, and put on his coat. Carefully he went to his closet and took down the one remaining article of clothing: a black homburg. He went to the bathroom mirror and studied himself exactingly as he placed it on his curly black bead. For a second, turning his head from side to side, he admired it, but knew he was admiring himself more. The hat didn't quite suit him; not yet.

He still wasn't quite up to its style. His Irish face was a little too heavy, almost jowly, which offset the ascetic poetry of his fine nose and fine black eyes. He was a handsome young man all right, but still not quite a gentleman. The hat said this. But it was good for a disguise. He would wear it out, just as he had worn it in five days ago. Then some wastebasket in some other neighborhood. The hat had served its purpose; two hotels were about all any diversion wearing apparel was good for. Anyway, it would make some poor slob of an ashcan-picker happy, and besides, he hadn't paid for it.

## III

"What are you doing?" Gloria called idly. She herself was touching up her nails with an emery board, a pursuit which she followed in almost every moment of leisure when Steve was not around. When he was around there was nothing doing; he said it made him sick, grated on his nerves, and that the colors she chose in nail polish wouldn't exist if prostitution was really stamped out. Though he wasn't nice about it, in a way he was quite funny. That was Steve: violent in his convictions great and small as a revolutionary, and rather amusing to watch. She didn't quite take him seriously.

Ellen appeared at the bathroom door, her head bundled up in a huge terrycloth towel.

"What, again?" Gloria remarked, meaning Ellen's hair washing habits—a thing that also got on Steve's nerves. He said if there was anything he hated it was an obvious guilt complex.

"It needed it this time, honest," Ellen said in her thin silvery Southern voice. It was a child's voice, and the one sure-fire thing, so Stephen said, which made Ellen's future in the theater assured. He admired it genuinely, so much so that it seemed to Gloria he would have liked to steal that too.

She smiled at Ellen. "Go on, kid," she chided. "I know you washed it day before yesterday."

"New York's a dirty ole place," Ellen replied, and it was as if a delicate clock had chimed.

Gloria smiled, and gave a small sigh of secret satisfaction. But she didn't harp on it. She had said her piece long since: "I just love to hear you talk, Ellen," was her one accolade to this beautiful voice belonging to this thin, silvery blonde wisp of a Southerner. The girl, of course, was pretty too, but her youngness maybe—something, something not quite formed, like baby bones, was lesser than the voice. The voice was like a haunting tender sound in the night, a beautiful polished instrument, a harp, maybe. Something like that. But belonging to Ellen the same way an heirloom necklace might; it was something her family had simply given her. She didn't ask how or why, or even its worth. She simply had it. Maybe Steve was right in wishing he could steal it. Gloria would rather like to steal it herself.

She looked up and noticed that Ellen had sat down at the desk and was all hunched over. This meant one of two things: either she was writing another of those unfinished, explanatory letters to her family, or she was silently crying. Gloria, having decided that she knew what Ellen was up to, went back to her nails. "I wouldn't try no more of them letters yet awhile," she said not unkindly. "If I was you."

Ellen's listlessness rolled back momentarily like a fog, and Gloria saw her eyes light in anger. She did not want either Gloria or Steve to interfere in her inner struggle about her family. "I am simply letting my hair stay like this five minutes," she said, her voice thin as spun glass but not unpleasant, however, because of its peculiar quality. "I am following the directions on this new shampoo."

"Oh," said Gloria quietly, but not at all chastened. She was much too even-tempered for that. She regarded Ellen's back; it was very young and rigid under the thin material of her robe, like a young birch. But an angry one, Gloria reflected. Well, in a way, she did not blame her. Steve was much too suspicious. And why should she, Gloria, "keep an eye" on Ellen in the first place? She wasn't the kid's keeper, or whatever. Sometimes "keeping an eye" made her feel like an odd combination of prison matron and kidnapper. If she ran out on them, or went to the cops—well, she had a right, didn't she? Anyway, Gloria didn't think she would. Ellen had a helluva lot more stuff than Steve gave her credit for. "This is some classy layout," Gloria observed lazily, her eyes traveling over the room as leisurely as if they were being carried for her. "He gets grander all the time. Next thing you know he'll be checking in at the White House."

"This place costs $25 a day," Ellen said without moving. "I'm reading the rate card. They've got it here on the desk. Under glass. Hah!"

Gloria laughed too, getting the joke. "Yeah, it's so expensive I guess they think somebody'd even steal that."

"That's just for a single," Ellen said, still as unmoving as cattle, determined to let her hair dry just so. "This room's in the $40 and up."

"Jesus Christ!" Gloria exclaimed, getting to her feet and throwing down the emery board as if it were something as large and effective as a tennis racket. "How much does that bastard think we can lift in a day?"

Ellen gave an almost invisible shrug. "I don't know the first thing that goes on in Mr. Stephen McCoy's so-called mind."

Gloria gazed at her a moment, then picked up her emery board and sat down. She knew that tone, all right, and she wasn't getting into *that* again. Stephen said Ellen was ambivalent about him; she thought he was God and the Devil rolled into one, except the two elements usually weren't rolled into one, and that was the trouble. They had had long talks about Ellen, even before they took off on this trip together. Gloria knew Ellen had him bugged; at least in a way. He was as ambivalent, on his side, as Ellen was on hers.

Usually Gloria didn't spend her time wondering and musing about other people's business—their families and all—unless it was some john with dough who was about to cut her in on a few bucks. But being with Ellen like this, day after day as they had been now for a couple of months, got her fascinated. Ellen didn't talk too much about it—oh, sometimes something here and there, little things about her kid brother, or the kind of flowers they had in their gardens, or the time she swiped the family Cadillac and that was how she learned to drive. But most of the concrete part she had got from Steve.

Ellen was from some hick town in the South—something North Carolina, population 7,000—and her old man had been a sort of bum, living off Ellen's family who were aristocrats and ashamed of him, until he got a violent case of religion. And now he was one of the biggest evangelists in that whole part of the country. Just rolling in jack. How his wife's family liked him now, Steve couldn't say, but it was pretty clear he ruled the roost; was one of those sons-of-bitches who roared and thundered in the pulpit against liquor, fast driving, loose women—the works—though he'd been one of the Lord's worst offenders in his time. The usual bit. But just how this affected Ellen's life at home, Gloria didn't know. But it must have been rough. She did say once that her father wouldn't allow her to go to her own cousins' houses because they had bridge parties and went to dances. So how had Ellen ended up at the University of Chicago? Maybe it was her mother's family's doings. Anyway, she was a pretty mixed-up kid, that was a fact, and small wonder.

Steve and Ellen had met at the university because they were both taking drama courses, and things like that. And Gloria knew the reason he'd been able to persuade Ellen to come away with them was because her old man had found out she was studying for the wicked theater and had threatened to take her out of school. So instead she had cut out with them. Maybe he had even disowned her, Gloria didn't know. But she knew Steve was worried

that her father might be having Ellen followed. All very dramatic—
Still, she'd never forget the look on Steve's face the second day out
on the road when Ellen admitted she was as broke as they were.
He thought she'd had a pile of dough all of her own—why, Gloria
didn't know in the face of all the other. But Stephen was also a
dramatic man.

She cast another thorough look at Ellen's back, saw that she
bad removed the headdress, and was sitting as patiently as before,
but her shoulders seemed to sag. The kid wasn't looking too well;
she needed to gain weight. And she was obviously worried. "It
seems to me," she said cheerfully, "that it's about time Steve let us
put up somewhere for a five-day rest instead of him staying the
same place five days in a row all the time.

"Yes," Ellen nodded. "Does he think we don't know we're
doing all the work? All he does is just take the stuff back." She
paused, as if putting their activities into words gave her a twinge of
physical pain, not just moral.

"We're really supporting the bastard," Gloria observed lightly,
no resentment in her tone. "We're saps."

"I wish it were no worse than just being saps," Ellen replied in
a husky whisper that had a disquieting effect on her listener.

"Well, time to get dressed," Gloria announced cheerily, standing up and yawning. "Hair about ready?"

IV

"You go on," Ellen said. "I'm not going."

The smile fell off Gloria's face as if it were a bright leaf leaving a tree. "Now, look here, honey—"

"I know, I know," Ellen said, her voice quite pleasant, almost charming. She appeared to be in the best of humors. "But I'm not all the same. Steve can plan—you know that, Gloria—without either one of us. He doesn't need me tonight. I just don't feel like it. Besides, it's cold out. I'll get something up from room service."

Gloria had a peculiar expression on her face, as if she suddenly suffered from frostbite, and couldn't think how or why. Ellen watched Gloria's indecision in friendly amusement, fully aware that she was putting on an act, one she might have to put off again. The tacit understandings that went on between the three about each other were like a whole library in braille—nothing you could see, but plenty you could feel. Would Gloria insist? Would she? She gazed steadily at Gloria, still assuming her smiling air of poise.

"Okay, kid," Gloria sighed, far from understanding, but agreeable to lending Ellen her sympathy. "But Steve won't like it." She couldn't resist this addition.

Ellen shrugged, and the two girls gazed at each other; not appraisingly, but as animals who share the same house sometimes regard their fellow captives.

"You're not sick?" Gloria's apprehension sounded strongly maternal.

Ellen shook her head. "Just tired—and, as I say, Steve can plot our course without me. Tell him I'll be a good girl," she added with

31

a smirk, and Gloria swiftly nodded, for this assurance from Ellen was as vital as a password if she was to get through the evening alone with Steve, without a storm. But Gloria wondered about it. She couldn't figure the kid out. Usually she was dying to get through the day so she could see Steve—sometimes he even took her back to his hotel with him. Gloria had thought Ellen lived for it. Maybe she was wrong. But what did Gloria know about twenty-year-old kids from the South, those with proper upbringings?

"Go on, cut out of here," Ellen urged her as if she were making a little joke with her best school pal.

Gloria, who was taller than Ellen, and who weighed at least twenty pounds more, found herself being propelled toward the bathroom, ever so lightly, Ellen's thin almost ghostly arm under Gloria's elbow.

"Lay off," Gloria said in slight annoyance, feeling like something of a fool. "Lover boy ain't in no rush."

Ellen laughed, and said, "Lover boy, my foot! Tell him I'm mad at him for sticking us in this expensive place."

Gloria turned to gaze at her, wondering if she really was all right, or was maybe brooding about something. Or maybe she even had something up her sleeve. Maybe it wasn't good sense to leave her all to herself. If anything happened— "Look here, kid," she started, then stopped. Ellen's eyes had a funny dead look in them, pale as ashes, the same delicate faded blue eyes as a very old woman who has seen everything and is now ready to stop looking at anything further. Gloria didn't like it. Ellen's eyes, no matter what her mood. were usually clear pretty eyes, as young as her years, pure, like a serene sky in the morning. "I'm not going either," Gloria said. "I don't feel so good."

"Oh, you faker!" Ellen crowed as if Gloria had just made a huge joke. She bent over in soundless laughter, and puzzled, Gloria watched her.

Quickly Ellen straightened up and went over and began to run a tub for Gloria. She sailed out of the bathroom and Gloria heard her clicking the locks on a suitcase. "Where's he meeting us to-night? Same place?" she called.

"Us?" echoed Gloria. "I thought you weren't coming."

"I'm not. I just thought I'd pick out a dress for you." Almost immediately she reappeared, holding Gloria's favorite cocktail dress; one they had swiped at Saks' and had kept, for Gloria couldn't bear to have Steve return it despite the sizeable amount of cold cash the price tag had indicated would be gained. She was touched that Ellen had chosen this particular dress for her, and took it as a sign of a growing friendship between them.

"Thanks, honey," she said warmly, and gave her friend a wink. "I'll knock 'em dead tonight. Who knows what'll happen?"

"Who knows?" Ellen replied and left the room as Gloria started wriggling out of her clothes to step into the tub.

When she was sure Gloria was actually in the tub, when the sounds of splashing were vigorous enough, she gave a small sigh of satisfaction and sank down into an easy chair, her arms indo-lently stretched along those of the chair, her hands hanging idle like two empty small gloves while she contemplated the room. She hadn't told either of them—having learned in the last weeks the value of keeping one's own counsel—that this was the very same hotel where she and her mother had stopped on their trip to New York during spring vacation last year; and they had shared a room similar to this. What a difference in roommates! She shook her head from side to side against the back of the eiderdown cushion; she was filled with mirth that was, all the same, close to grief. Irony it was not; that was too corny, but tears and laughter were hotly compounded and she felt on the verge of passionate action. If only that well-meaning whore would get out of here!

She got up and strode around, her steps broad for so frail a girl, and vigorous, purposeful. She surveyed the room. Very nice.

When Gloria came out of the bath, Ellen had again sunk down in her easy chair, still dressed in her robe, her hair now lemony yellow, being half dry, instead of the birch silver it would finally be, and was absorbed in a book she had found; an anthology especially collected and published for this particular hostelry. She was grinning to herself over the selections, turning the pages as she read, savoring each line heartily.

Gloria glanced at her as she got into her slip, thinking how alike Stephen and Ellen were in some ways (even though he was common like herself). They got the same look on their faces when they were reading, for instance, a sort of superiority look as if they were mentally making fun of the author. Of course Stephen had told Gloria that Ellen was very bright, had a high I.Q. and all, and maybe it was so. Gloria couldn't really tell. They were certainly three strange bedfellows all right, which was a laugh, since that's exactly what they were—or had been from time to time—until Ellen got squeamish about it.

"Zip me?" Gloria requested, putting it in such a way to make it sound as if she expected to be refused.

Ellen got up and zipped up the back of Gloria's dress, and Gloria, gowned and coiffed, perfumed and painted, ready to go, made for the full-length mirror in the bathroom door, walking in that entranced dream-state of all beautiful people bound for a look at their own breath-taking vision, prepared and yet excited all over again for what was in store. Her eyes, slightly hooded, through the habit of years of sensual excitation, her hips undulant beneath the silk of her clinging dress. As she approached, Ellen watched her draw in her breath and stare with awe and satisfaction at what she saw. Now Gloria sucked in her mouth slightly, a model's trick, making her high cheekbones more prominent, her good bone structure appear better, and pursed the wide, brazenly rich red mouth. Her survey was not so much an appraisal as an invitation, as if some man waited on the other side of the looking-glass. Again she saw Gloria lower her eyes at a voluptuous half-mast before she was willing to take leave of herself. Ellen turned aside. It was too much like catching Narcissus at his pool, and yet Gloria was one of the least consciously vain women she'd ever met. It was, put in Gloria's tough, honest and sensible way, simply that she liked "to look good" and "get a kick out of life."

Fleetingly, Ellen looked at her own reflection which, admittedly, was hardly ready for display. But even so she thought: I look tender; a green shoot, and left the mirror to absorb merely the hotel-luxuriousness of the quiet room, free now of herself or of Gloria, the latter having gone to get her coat from the closet. "I'll probably freeze in this old horse blanket," Gloria muttered in disgust. "I wish I could cop me a mink."

Ellen gave her a laugh as cool and silvery as bells on the winter air, and with a backward laugh, Gloria went out the door, thinking to herself: I'm gonna have me some fun tonight, and was rather glad Ellen hadn't come along. If worse came to worse she'd even go back to spend the night with Stephen. Ellen didn't own him; she, Gloria, had as much right to him as Ellen did.

V

This intention was precisely what Ellen had surmised as Gloria had gone out the door. It was unmistakably there, brief but as certain as a whiff of perfume. Thoughtfully, Ellen considered it. Of course Stephen wouldn't mind. She had an idea he and Gloria often sneaked off for little matinees, when they could take time off from their work. Their "work"! She threw herself on her bed and laughed until she was sobbing.

Then she sat up, finding her unhappiness completely untenable in this form. It was like getting hysterics while swimming and consequently drowning because you couldn't help gulping water when you laughed. Either you got out of the water or you lost your sense of humor if you wanted to live. Getting out of the water was no mean trick; especially if you hadn't bothered to count the fathoms on the way down. It had all seemed so different—so awful—so ludicrous—so irresistible until she had first hit bottom. That had been on the first night away from Chicago. At Stephen's suggestion they had stayed in some snazzy hotel. He had shared a room with her and Gloria was off to herself. But, as it had worked out, Gloria had made a buck or two all the same, for the hotel had spotted her immediately, their motto apparently being waste not, want not, just as in some ordinary dump. If Ellen had gone in doe-eyed, as she had heard Stephen describe her look in the state of love, she had come out fox-eyed. For up until then, flaming and obviously bottled red hair or not, she had not really believed that Gloria was merely a common trollop. She had, despite her natural suspicions, taken Stephen's word for it: according to him, Gloria was a tough but beautiful kid, on her own since she was fourteen when she had run away from her sharecropper family in Oklahoma, and that she had since made her living as an artists' model and occasionally singing cool jazz with the combos in the small clubs. Stephen had even admitted that they had gone to bed together once or twice, but that, he said, was all over; they were just pals, real pals.

With her new knowledge Ellen began to wonder how broad the term "real pals" was in Stephen's meaning. Had he had any visible sign of support, over and beyond his thin GI allowance? No. Yet he was what her Southern mammy back home would have described as "a big spender." And Gloria's clothes were not cheap, however flashy. When she was introduced to Ellen she had even been wearing a cerulean mink stole.

So that morning when he told her with disarming candor, as the three of them sat at the first of their round-table breakfasts, that he and Gloria were "flat for the moment" and couldn't afford to continue the trip, except by hitchhiking, Ellen had let the unfinished sentence ravel off into nowhere, the broad hint disappearing with it. Finally, as they both looked at her alertly, she had shrugged and said, "I guess it's hitchhiking then." And that was the day she had torn up her checkbook, as she knew now that Stephen was more than just clever, and she wanted no evidence around as to her true financial worth.

They had gone to the edge of town, trudging along now as the fall weather was unseasonably warm and their suitcases (the girls carried their own) as heavy as if they carried the hot sun in them. The act of moving along the pavement made conversation an added burden, so Ellen had time all to herself for facing her net of despair. After all, I'm only twenty, was the only self-exoneration she could summon to mind, accompanied by the excuses of having had a sheltered Southern life, and a torn one. It was so hard, she found, not to be silly. She felt more like singing snatches of meaningless tunes, Ophelia-style, than thinking things through. Her fingers toyed with the wires of her net instead of tearing at them.

Before their first ride came she had managed to sift through the facts at hand in a haphazard vague fashion; had found enough to let her persuade herself to go on this mad enterprise. She was in love with Stephen, no matter what he did; she was sick of school and family and wanted desperately to be in New York on her own and see if she really did have the talent she believed she had. What better way to do it? In any event, if ever she was to give herself a chance it would mean running away, just as she was doing now. She had started it, why not go on? But she was determined in going on that she would not be used. It would have to be share and share alike. If Stephen loved her, he would help her. There was, she felt, something very fine in him, covered over though it was by this sordidness which made him team up his gentle sweetheart with a whore. Perhaps it appealed to his sense of irony and adventure; she confessed that it did to hers, however great her distaste for Gloria.

Looking back on it now, she knew she had never "hated" Gloria. She had been fiercely murderous toward her the night the three of them had sex together—at Stephen's connivance—when all of them had been forced by circumstance to share the same bed. That night she had rebelled, wept and reviled. She had pulled out all the stops; had made a fool of herself and had gained no point. Using some of her father's oratory and certainly his power at self-hypnotism, she had called on the Almighty to witness their carnal sin and punish them. Gloria and Stephen had been frightened and fascinated, but Stephen had roughly shut her up. Now, remembering it, she wondered if her puritanical strain was as strong as all that, or had it been histrionics? Ellen's mother, an Episcopalian by birth, was a disinterested agnostic by practice, but a quiet one and therefore not a hindrance to her father's affairs. Wasn't Ellen somewhat like her? Certainly, she believed, as did her mother, that a religious experience was first of all vulgar. However, these were private thoughts, and remained unshared with her teammates. They, she knew, thought she marinated in the tortuous waters of original sin, loathing every minute of her defection, being dragged along by them, unwilling but will-less like a wet sheet being fed into a wringer.

The truth was that she was not so against the sinning as she was shy, not so stubborn as she was awkward. Living the sort of life Stephen and Gloria had doped out for them actually rather appealed to Ellen; it was ingenious and therefore stimulating. But putting it into practice was another thing. It always sounded divinely exciting while the three were mapping out plans, took on the aspect of a huge practical joke, but one that all three should know was really too mean to do. Yet when the doing time came, neither Gloria nor Stephen seemed to find it too mean. They went about it not so cold-bloodedly as surgically. Ellen tried to emulate their detachment, but she steamed with false compassion, as Stephen had called it. This led, inevitably, to their tutoring of her, as if she were a dumb pupil.

Thinking that her recalcitrance was of religious origin, they both gave her long spirited lessons on the nature of good and evil as opposed to right and wrong. Gloria, a natural heathen, was proud of the fact that she had learned about religion in the same way some dirty little boy had instructed her about sex. She had found it as interesting, but as unlikely. That God was watching her from Heaven seemed as unbelievable as the rumor that babies were gotten by boys and girls doing that funny thing to each other. "Have you ever watched a pigeon tread?" asked Stephen, the fallen-away Catholic.

But Ellen had pointed out, more to confound Gloria than anything else, that indeed babies were gotten by doing that funny thing; ergo, by her logic, there was a god in a heaven watching them sin. Gloria had sighed, but Stephen had laughed, rather pleased with Ellen; then he had gone back to his original thesis of good and evil which had nothing to do with right and wrong. Retail business, he said, was legalized robbery. Making a profit was morally wrong, inhumane. Didn't Ellen see that? Therefore, using the Robin Hood law, a truly moral person was almost obligated to steal.

"Shit," was Gloria's comment, tired of the endless indoctrination, "either she sees it or she don't. Anyway, me, I'm not fixin' to starve, and if I have to feed me by hustlin' or liftin' or anything 'wrong' like that, well, I'll just be wrong—and evil."

Their design for living in New York had evolved as necessity demanded. The shoplifting had come first, at Gloria's suggestion, and she had taught them both, being an old-time master at it herself. She taught them the trick of making a small purchase in a given store (always an expensive one) in order to learn exactly how the price tag was processed—torn or marked. The rest was easy; it consisted simply in stealing an item, preferably light and easily concealed, later fixing the price tag and eventually returning it to the credit department for cash, saying the sales slip had been lost. Stephen added a few fine points to this; the chief one being his role in the routine. Reasonably he showed them that a man should make the returns, for it was easier to convince a credit manager that a male would never think of retaining a sales slip on a purchase he had made as a gift to his wife. So Gloria and Ellen took over the actual theft. They were both careful and adroit, never stealing from the same store more than once or twice. Though this limited the time-period their "livelihood" could last, for even New York does not have an endless number of high quality stores, they all preferred it this way. The danger of being caught was very slight, and anyway, hadn't they all come to New York with other purposes in mind? Gloria, to land *the* rich john who would eternally keep her, or at least settle a lot of money on her not to; Stephen, to finish his masterpiece and get it published; and Ellen to seriously go on the stage. These amoral activities they indulged in now meant nothing; just a stopgap until they got going.

Ellen did not buy this exactly (after all, she did have money in the bank and could have lived otherwise), but she wanted to hang on to Stephen; moreover, her new life had an addictive quality; she gulped "experience" as if her whole past existence had been spent in a parched desert. For this reason, she knew she was the immoral one of the three. It bothered her intermittently.

Oddly enough, the hotel racket, which had been the result solely of Stephen's fertile mind, bothered her most. She had actually stayed, as a paying guest, in many of the hotels they visited, for her parents had made frequent trips to New York on which she had been brought along. She was not so literal-minded or conceited as to think the hotel personnel would recognize her, but in these familiar lobbies and suites she recognized herself. Gloria and Stephen could detect her depressions, but couldn't explain them. She was as enigmatic in her moods as a thermometer; she simply registered her spiritual weather, but did not explain it. For instance, neither Stephen nor Gloria ever knew when one of the hotels they checked into had been the scene of a childhood sightseeing visit for Ellen. They explained her moroseness on the grounds of conscience and cowardice, almost fondly respecting her depressions, for being a "nice girl" she had all the novelty of a peek-show for them, and they were more or less pleased to be allowed to look on.

But this was only part of it. Actually, the hotel game was exceedingly risky, though so far it had worked smooth as glass. All three recognized it as the desperate remedy it was, and Gloria and Stephen, at least, had a daredevil attitude toward it. It had come about soon after they arrived, when the three were again sharing the same room, but quite primly so in order to cater to Ellen's sense of propriety and property, and all of them felt the strain. Though the shoplifting had gotten into gear, they still had to conserve funds, and living all in a clump, with no privacy, oppressed them. They felt impoverished financially and sexually. Stephen, who had a strong lust for both girls, though each in entirely different ways, had grown sullen and testy, and the resentment between Ellen and Gloria was drawing to a focus. The hotel plan saved them. As usual, Stephen planned it to his own comfort-loving advantage, and, as usual, on reasonable grounds. He outlined the mechanics for them, during one of their after-shoplifting-hours sessions which they had come to call campaign meetings or skull practice. He, Stephen, would check into a hotel under an assumed name, taking adequate baggage with him so that he would not be asked to pay in advance. After the five-day period usually allowed a guest before financial pressure in a good hotel, he would quietly disappear, leaving his door unlocked. The girls meantime would have checked in for an overnight stay, preferably in a room on the same floor. They would go to his room, collect his luggage, and that would be that. Luggageless for that night only, he would check into some cheap place. The next day all three would check out of their hotels, and Stephen would pick up his luggage from a locker in Grand Central Station where the girls had taken it. He would then, as Louis Carrol, or Fletcher Beaumont, or some other gifted composite, check into a new hotel and start all over again. All of which was fine for him.

For Ellen and Gloria it was not so fine. It meant they had only one decent night's lodging out of every five, but, as Stephen pointed out, look at the money they saved. Gloria and Ellen, for four nights every week, lived in and paid for a shabby room on the West Side—their headquarters. And on their fifth night out they still had to pay, while Stephen, once around the circle, paid the equivalent of a cell in the YMCA. It was he, also, who rigidly insisted that everyone pay his own way—except, of course, their income which came from shoplifted goods was divvied up three ways, though nobody seriously credited Stephen with having done a third of the work. As might also be expected, he insisted that he was entitled to what he got, being the Brain.

Tonight was the first time Ellen had missed one of the nightly get-togethers, though of late they had been little more than inspirational pep-talks by Stephen, administered like candy to children, to keep the girls in line. He hadn't even mentioned the relationship between them for weeks—the thing that had drawn Ellen into this in the beginning. At first she had yearned, then she had worried, then she had cooled into listlessness. That she still loved, wanted, and needed him stood out naked and shameless, and she knew that if the phone rang this instant (most unlikely as it was dangerous) she would rush off to join them.

She looked at the phone, a white one, stunning in its pristine, expensive aspect, an exactly right choice for the decor of the room, and strengthened her determination. She had other uses for it besides talking to Stephen, and nothing spur-of-the-moment either. Since she had gone to the trouble of coming to New York to get somewhere, that was where she was going to get, and no more wasting time.

## VI

Except for one small and rather expensive bar in the Village, located far from the hotel circuit uptown and further insured for safety because of its clientele—the less obvious lesbians and a handful of very elegant snobbish male homosexuals whose noses and manners were commensurate with their high salaries—the partnership had no regular meeting place. Instead, from night to night they varied their spots from East Side to West, from dive to decorum, depending on Stephen's whimsical mood or impeccable judgment. He enjoyed the cloak and daggerism of their existence, and paid as much meticulous attention to furtive detail and caution as any smart criminal. Gloria was a quick and astute second in command, never questioning, as Ellen frequently did And it wasn't simply that Ellen was new to it all.

Instead it was a matter of disposition and insight, Stephen had concluded. Gloria, though she had had no schooling to speak of, and certainly had not taken any courses in logic and semantics at the University of Chicago, still had what he liked to call "dead reckoning." He considered her the purest vein of mother-wit he had ever found, but, like any canny prospector, kept this find to himself. And though Gloria had a vague idea that he admired her for more than her looks and practical talents, she had never guessed how deeply he respected her opinions, or how exactly he usually acted on them.

It was through her offices on this particular night that Ellen's caprice would be tolerated, and Gloria banked heavily on this. But the anticipation made her nervous.

When she reached their Village meeting place, which had been agreed upon the night before, she was amazed to find that Stephen, the stickler for punctuality, was nowhere in sight. She took a place at the bar, crossed her legs and looked around, unconsciously assaying the place, though her mind was on Stephen's lateness. She found herself glancing nervously toward the door each time it opened, and was reminded of Ellen who sometimes door-watched this way, if they happened to arrive a few minutes early; she reminded Gloria of a dog dumbly aching for the presence of its master. Or something worse—something murky and marine in the way Ellen's eyes darted frantically toward the door, as if her eyes were minnows seeking food or escape. What a fool to love a guy so much, especially something like Stephen. She averted her own glance from the door and trained it on a group well to the back of the room. But her attention would not fasten there, though the people looked interesting, obviously strangers to the place for habitues sat up front or at the bar. What gives with us? is what she thought. What is all this?

First of all Ellen had mysteriously begged off coming, and now Stephen was late. Two unprecedented events. Was the three-way operation on the rocks? It had better not be. She was not ready for it to be; she needed both of them. She needed Ellen, she freely admitted, as a buffer against Stephen. Of late he had made far too many surreptitious hints about Ellen's being a tiresome burden, and why didn't they scuttle her. Gloria knew he didn't quite mean it, but at the same time she knew, as she had always known, that if she gave Stephen a real tumble, he would go serious on her. And she wasn't about to support *him* while he wrote the Great American Novel, which, of course, would inevitably be part of the bargain. Anyway, there were many things about Stephen she did not personally like. He represented a coarse streak which was duplicated in herself. Like too much chuck in a side of beef—good for little or nothing except sham as something else, or toughness for its own sake. With Stephen she might fall back into her origin, and lose whatever grace she had acquired. And again Ellen had her uses: she was constantly learning from her, she felt. And one day, if left time to develop along the lines her pride dictated, she would land that john, and what's more she would even know how to make him marry her. But would there be time? Was Stephen going to stand her up, and if so, what for?

With failing hope, her mind swift as an archer stepped in, took aim and hit the target with a piercingly logical answer, he'd found something better to do. God no! she cried almost aloud.

What a fool she had been to elude him all these weeks! Why not give it away, since she wasn't selling it? She'd never minded before. But somehow until tonight, when she had made her mind up to go back to his place with him if he asked, she just plain hadn't wanted to. Nor did she really now, but that infallible eighth or ninth sense of hers had earlier sent the dictate to her mind, as if in warning. Okay. But what if he didn't show?

Her eyes drifted back to the group at the rear. They had been having dinner; the dishes were now being cleared. She focused her interest on them like a spy with a telescope, her excellent vision reporting the fact that they were now having liqueurs—nothing in itself; anybody with a dollar or two in his jeans could have a brandy or a creme de menthe, but these weren't jeans. These people, two women, three men, were dressed. The men were in dinner jackets, the women in evening dresses—one with a chinchilla draped over the back of her chair, like in that fancy liquor advertisement. Gloria glanced anxiously away from them and back toward the door. Live ones, yet! But without Steve she couldn't really do a thing.

Her eyes were irresistibly drawn back to the party, like a hungry person's to a feast. It had been a long time since she had flushed such a covey, and she watched them as if she were some strange breed of animal whose entire subsistence depends on crisp, green currency. She took careful stock of her game, like a hunter looking through his sights. The women were two old painted hags, she noted in cool dismissal; they had wattles for throats, and the flesh sagged obscenely from the armpits of their expensive dresses. She could just imagine their breasts, worn-out milk bags! Poor guys. But they weren't. They were all young—or old-young, and these dames were either their mothers, their rich aunts, or, God forbid, their wives. If only that damn Steve would come!

He strode up behind her. "Sorry," he said crisply, his presence behind her cool and new-minted as his voice. He was like the weather outside and yet had the pampered redolent smell of men's toiletries. Ellen had once pointed out that she found him, in this condition, vastly attractive, but now all Gloria could find to recommend him was his presence.

"Where's our Southern cornpone? In the john?" he asked insidiously, curving toward her, his cool overcoat sleeve administered rather like a rag soaked with chloroform. Gloria sat erect.

"Ellen didn't come," she said, and filled in the details. Before she could stop him, he had gone off toward the phone booth. Hurriedly she went after him.

"Don't," she begged. "Let her alone. Anyway, I wanted to see you tonight." The way she put it made him know she meant alone, and he hung up the phone receiver, got his coin, and trailed her back to the bar like an enraptured sultan stalking a prospect for his harem. He sat down beside her and grinned.

"Are you hungry?" she asked.

"Are you?" he answered slyly, leaving no doubt that his reply referred to something other than just food.

She cut her eyes away and laughed a little. "Oh, Steve," she said, then looked squarely at him. "Baby, we love it, don't we?"

"You bet we do," he said, his voice husky, the grin on his face now rather ugly with unrestrained desire.

"There's lots in the back—money, I mean," she said, dipping her head down to watch the drink she whirled in its glass; and, as she thought, the bait worked. Stephen turned his head sharply.

"I see The March of Time," he said.

"I see tempus fugiting," she said, her voice as alluring and suggestive as a curve. And he smiled, just as she knew he would: Steve was always a pushover for that pseudo-literary kind of gag. "Shall we dine in the rear?" she added, rising.

He took her elbow, squeezing it slightly, and pointing it as if it were some ancient weapon of defense. It annoyed her, but she simply smiled. "Those old dames," she said, inclining her head toward his ear, "look like they could use a bright young man like you."

"And if they can't?" he whispered back, his breath warm on her cheek.

"There's always home-folks," was her answer.

He brushed his mouth against hers, then straightened, and guided Gloria to a table at the back.

Johnny, who waited on the tables in that section, came over for their order. "Where's the little girl *ce soir*?" Johnny asked. Johnny was a dancer and a bit TV actor who had spent a year in Europe; no one seemed to know whether he was a girl or boy, and no one they knew seemed interested enough to take Stephen's suggestion of turning Johnny upside down to find out.

"She's sick," Gloria said and studied the menu avidly, as if she had never seen it before.

Stephen's expression was bored. "Steak," he said shortly.

"Make it two. Rare."

"Wait," Gloria said. "I'm hungry tonight. I want something to start with."

"Well, make up your mind," Stephen said impatiently.

"That's all right, dear. I've got all night," Johnny said in a way that made it sound like the truth rather than sarcasm.

"I haven't," Stephen rasped.

Gloria gave him a long look which he missed. Stephen's disposition was as changeable as April. Now, what was the matter with him? She ordered, and Johnny, before he sauntered away, fingered the sleeve of her dress admiringly. "You look real good tonight, hon," he said.

"Beat it!" said Stephen ominously.

Johnny gave him an arched-eyebrow look of disdain, and left, taking his time.

"Jesus, I can't stand those—"

Gloria gave him a warning look and barely inclined her head toward the group at the table nearby. If he blew his top he might scare them away.

"I don't know why you and Ellen like these hotbeds of pansies," he growled.

She didn't bother to answer him: the place was, as he very well knew, his own discovery. Instead, she turned her face directly toward him, so that her profile, which was excellent, was on full display for the group beyond. Then, when she had held the pose long enough, she turned her face again, and flashed a radiant smile at her escort, projecting it as if the group beyond were a movie screen. "Have they noticed us yet?" she asked in an undertone, her lips as unmoving asa ventriloquist's.

Stephen, who had been watching them under heavy brows, continued to scowl slightly, but Gloria knew the storm had come and gone. "Yup," he answered.

"How about the big one? The one with the sort of crew cut?"

"He's watching you, but he's getting up. I think they're ready to leave."

Gloria gave a small disappointed sigh, but bravely kept face.

After an interval she turned to look at them. Two of the men were helping the women with their coats. Then the women went off in the direction of the Ladies' Room.

While they were gone, Gloria took full and bold advantage of their absence. Now the hooded, seductive look in her eyes was replaced by a wide-open stare, not so much an invitation as a challenge—a trick she had picked up from Lauren Bacall movies. Her eyes, she knew, in this particular light would shine with the liquid softness of gems, and against her skin, they would be like dark fiery stones set in creamy velvet. She was aware that Stephen was watching her in amusement; even back in Chicago he had always liked to watch her work.

When the women rejoined their companions, Gloria turned back to Stephen. "Okay?"

"You hooked 'em," he said wryly. "All of 'em. Now what are you going to do? Have a daisy chain?"

Gloria laughed happily. "Did you get your old dame?" she asked.

"Who knows?" Stephen shrugged. "I gave Grandmother Chinchilla my boyish grin."

Detached and sure of themselves, Gloria and Stephen watched the group leave; they knew the right ones would be back.

## VII

When Ellen got out of the cab at Gracie Square, she agreed with the driver that it was probably going to snow, collected her change and walked away in the direction of the apartment house where her cousins lived. She had her face tucked into the fur collar of her coat, the tips of the fur tickling her cheek as if the animal were alive and playful. As she walked, she breathed deeply in and out; it was good air, and somehow this neighborhood up here made her think of home. It had trees and things, and was quiet, the way a residential part of town should be. But in New York such an atmosphere was a luxury, and only people like Ellen's family could afford it. She stopped for a moment and looked around in the twilight. The mayor's house looked like any nice house down home, and the trees looked down home too. They were bare now, and their branches dark against the silky gray sky were like cracks in a dark milk-glass bowl, forming the same kind of patterns as the prints of bird's feet. Pretty, she thought, but quite ugly too. She walked on, humming slightly to herself and wondering just what kind of tale she was going to tell her cousins.

She had called them when Gloria had left her by herself, and her cousins had instantly asked her to dinner tonight. Properly speaking, only Walter was her cousin, but his wife Courtney's brother was married to still another cousin who lived in Raleigh, so she had been regarded as part of the family even before Walt married her. The idea of calling them was in ordinary circumstances hardly her notion of fun, but it occurred to Ellen that seeing them might be useful, and besides it would be nice to see some decent people again. They were very decent indeed, very correct. They were in the *Social Register* and of course belonged to the Southern Club.

Walter Charlesworth was Ellen's second cousin on her mother's side, and was her mother's contemporary rather than hers; however, he was a few years younger and had gone around with a younger crowd when they were growing up. Since his marriage, he and Courtney had lived in New York, but went "down home" at least four or five times a year. Ellen couldn't remember a Christmas when Walter had not made the eggnog (unspiked in their house, of course, since her father "got the call"). He was a twinkly-eyed fun-loving man, and Ellen was fairly fond of him. He always told jokes and played pranks eternally. Courtney, on the other hand, was inclined to be sober-faced, but looked with fond tolerance on Walter's antics. However, Ellen did not really know them well. Though her mother usually telephoned them when she was in New York, and though both parties made a pretense of wanting to get together, they seldom did, for, of course, her father did not approve of them. The Charlesworths were "high livers" and drank.

Ellen smiled to herself thinking about them, and walked a little faster. She was glad now that she had called them, and knew she was lucky to find them in town, for Walter was a vice-president or something for some steel corporation and he was constantly away visiting his company's plants all over the country. Courtney usually went with him, as they had no children to tie her down.

Ellen turned in the doorway, and the doorman stepped back with her under the marquee, opening the huge heavy glass door, a look of polite inquiry on his face. "The Charlesworths," Ellen said rather curtly, and the doorman relayed the message to the elevator man, in full evening dress, white tie included, who waited to take her up.

Walter and Courtney lived in the penthouse, it seemed. Walter was at the door, drink in hand, when Ellen stepped out of the elevator. The doorman had telephoned up.

"Well, looka here at you," he beamed, putting an arm fondly around her shoulder and giving her cheek a noisy but almost contactless little peck. Courtney was right behind him, looking either shy or inhospitable, but her voice was warm as she greeted Ellen, and she kissed Ellen too.

"Let me have your coat," she said in her shy slow drawl.

"Here, Bubber," she said to her husband, handing him Ellen's coat, "you hang it up."

But "Bubber," as she affectionately called her husband, had moved out of the foyer and was in the warmly lighted living room, standing at a Jacobean chest, his back to them, pouring a drink. "I'll declare, you just aggravate me so!" Courtney surprisingly said, and Ellen watched mutely as Courtney hung the coat up herself. She wondered if they had been in the midst of an argument.

"Well, Cuz," Walter said brightly, turning to face Ellen as she tentatively walked into the living room, "you're looking good. Don't you think so, Suster?"

Ellen remembered that Walter teasingly called Courtney by this name, in retaliation for her calling him Bubber; now that she thought of it, it was absurd for husband and wife to be calling each other nicknames that stood for brother and sister. It occurred to her to wonder just what their relationship was—a curiosity she could never remember having had before about any other "grownup" members of her family. Heretofore they had all been just old and being just old meant that they were fixed in time more securely than stars, everything settled, all passion spent, which all spelled DULL in letters as high and dusty as an old house.

With new eyes, then, Ellen watched her cousins alertly, her face bright, her expression candid with eagerness.

"I always did think Ellen Tate Terrill was going to make a right pretty woman," Courtney replied, Southern as hush puppies, and giving Ellen's full name but one.

"That's sweet of you, Cousin Courtney," Ellen said, falling too. How easy to slip back into it!

Walt handed her a tumbler of bourbon on the rocks with a splash of the inevitable "branch water."

"Now, Bubber, how do you know she takes hers like that," his wife reproved him. "Maybe she doesn't take whisky at all."

"What?" Walt asked in pretended dismay, "a good North Carolinian, just full of Charlesworth blood who doesn't like a little taste before 'dunner'? I'm ashamed of you, Courtney."

Courtney did not look at all convinced, even though Ellen took the tumbler readily and gave her a reassuring smile.

"It's just Daddy," she said. "Mama likes an old-fashioned herself."

"See there, Suster, I told you!" Walter beamed triumphantly. "I've seen your mother take a little taste or two," he informed Ellen. "More than just a taste. Why one night right after Leta and your pappy got married—"

"Hush, Bubber," Courtney said. "And get that wicked look out of your eye."

"Oh, Daddy used to drink," Ellen affirmed. "I remember it, though at the time I was just a little baby."

"You're just a little baby now, sugar!" Walt said gleefully, and he did not notice that Ellen shot his wife an uncomfortable look.

"All this being settled," Courtney said somewhat sarcastically, "how about fixing me mine?"

"Oh, honey, not that. Why not just for tonight—"

"No, Bubber," she shook her head firmly. "I just want my special drink." She turned to Ellen, "He keeps trying to get me to liking 'bourbon,' but I'm sorry, I just can't abide the stuff. It just tastes *nasty* to me."

"What do you drink?" Ellen inquired politely, to continue this gracious confidence.

"She drinks vermouth," Walter said in disgust, "like they do in Italy."

"Well, Bubber, you used to drink it there yourself."

"That was different. They didn't have any real drinkin' whisky."

Courtney giggled, then said, "You know what he used to do in France, Ellen Tate Terrill? He got so tired of that ole Armagnac and cognac—what they call *fine*—that he used to drink it with Coca-Cola."

"Now, Courtney, you know you're just making that up," he complained. "You've told that story on me so much you actually believe it. I did it once. On a bet," he explained to Ellen, and added to his wife, "and you four-letter word well know it."

"Why, Walter Tate Charlesworth! If you aren't the biggest—"

"*Pas devant les domestiques*—" he suddenly cautioned in extremely flat French, and gestured toward an ebony figure in a white apron and cap grinning in the dining room archway. "*Tiens, tiens, tiens,*" he continued drolly, pretending astonishment. "*Quel surprise, ma belle, ma bonne,* my kitchen queen! This is Rastus Louise, Suster's French maid," he went on grabbing Ellen's hand and leading her over to the servant who now appeared to be dying with laughter. "Say a few words of French for Miss Madem-morsel, Rastus chile."

"I cain't speak no French, but I know what *you* talkin' about!" Rastus Louise recovered herself enough to say.

"Why, Bubber, you're just perfectly awful tonight!" Courtney, pretended to give him a little scolding tap on the shoulder, as light and coy as if she had done it with a fan. "I can't understand what's gotten into you."

"I'm showing off for my favorite cuz," he said, looking more than ever like a mischievous but large leprechaun.

"Doesn't Bubber speak just the worst French you ever heard?" Courtney wanted to know. "It's even worse than mine."

"That's because my English is so much better, so it's twice as hard to make it stay in its place when I'm supposed to be talking French. It gets jealous."

As they went into the dining room, Courtney told Ellen about the years they had spent in Europe, when Walter had been in charge of the Paris office; long before Ellen's time.

Dinner was very good and very jovial; they talked about other cousins and about other Southerners living in exile here in New York. Ellen got the feeling that she had never left home, but more strongly that they never had. They seemed to know nothing but fellow Southerners. It began to oppress her. Then, quite without warning, Courtney switched the subject to Ellen—her immediate present, not her comfortable past—and there was something in the way she did it that put Ellen immediately on guard.

"I thought spring vacation came at Eastertime," Courtney remarked. "It always did when I was at Randolph-Macon."

She gave Ellen a direct look while she daintily touched her napkin to her lips.

"Did I say spring vacation?" Ellen asked innocently. What a damn fool she had been to think she could blurt out just any old reason on the telephone when Walter had asked her what she was doing in New York. "I meant to say—I *thought* I said—I'd be coming back for spring vacation. I'm just in town for a few days-getting allergy shots," she added wildly.

"You poor thing!" Courtney exclaimed, aghast.

"Yes," Ellen lowered her eyes and went to work in earnest. "There's this specialist here—][ saw him last year with Mama—"

"I didn't know that," Courtney said, still astonished. "Why didn't Martha Lou write us about that, Bubber? I think that's just terrible!"

"It really is," Walter said quietly.

Ellen started to continue, but she noticed a funny look on Walter's face. He had averted his eyes when she looked at him. He knows it's a big fat lie, she thought. Good God! "Yes," she said, "but I'm having a good time anyway—buying clothes—"

"Seeing shows?" Courtney supplied.

"Well, that was one thing I wanted to ask you about. Isn't your cousin Ella's daughter playing in something on Broadway?"

"Um hm," Courtney nodded. She couldn't speak until she had swallowed the small forkful of peas. "Sissy's in *Speak of the Devil*. She's got a real big part, too. She took that what's-her-name's place who was in it at first—oh, you know who I mean. What's her name, Bubber?—and she's just fine. We're so proud of her. Bubber and I have seen the show I bet you twenty times. It's been running quite a while, you know. A real hit."

"Yes, I know," said Ellen.

"And Lord, the way that child studied! She studied and studied and *more* studied! Ella couldn't get her to take an interest in anything but the theater. She was determined to be a big star, and well, now it's paid off, and Ella's not so upset anymore because Sissy didn't want to go out with boys and go to dances and things—"

"Lord, Courtney, to hear you talk you'd think Sissy Blackburn was the divine Bernhardt," Walter put in.

"Well, she *is* good," Courtney said defensively.

"Does she use that name professionally?" asked Ellen who had never known of Sissy Blackburn's dramatic proclivities until her mother had casually mentioned it in a letter written months before while Ellen was still in Chicago.

"No," Courtney said, drawing out the word for emphasis. "She calls herself *Courtney* Blackburn."

"That's the reason we have to keep seeing the play," Walter

interjected teasingly.

"It most certainly is not. Courtney's her name as much as mine. We were both named after Great grandmother Courtney Childers."

"It's a good name for the stage," Ellen observed. "I wish mine were as good."

"You've got aspirations for the stage?" Walter inquired, not sure whether to make a joke of it or not.

Ellen nodded. "Daddy'd kill me if he knew. He thinks I'm going to be a teacher."

Courtney gave her a look of motherly sympathy. "What does Leta think about it?"

"Oh, mama doesn't think I'm serious. She thinks I'll grow out of it."

"Do they have a good drama department out there in Chicago?" Walter asked with seeming casualness.

"Better than the one at Sweet Briar—at least for me—that's where I first got interested in acting. When Daddy found out I'd been in just one little ole thing, he threw a fit."

"If I recollect, Frank Potts is pretty good at that," Walter commented.

His wife gave him a look of shock and horror.

Ellen laughed easily, however, and said, "Yes, Daddy's got a hot temper."

This time Walter made no comment, but opened up a new subject. "How come your mama let you go off to that Yankee school? Did you put your foot down and say, 'I'm going and there ain't no fool can stop me?'"

Ellen laughed at him. "Not hardly," she said, feeling that nothing but the colloquial double-negative could answer *that* one so well. "My best friend at Sweet Briar was going there, so I wanted to go there too. The only trouble is now we don't speak."

"Well, Lord love us, chile!" Walter exclaimed. "Hadn't you just better hightail it on back home then, and stop foolin' around with all those Yankees?"

"Now, Bubber stop it. You know Wellesley's a nice school, and Vassar too. There're lots of nice schools up North. Your own mother went to one."

"Not long, she didn't. She married Daddy instead."

"Well," said Courtney slowly, still satisfied that she had carried her point.

"I might transfer after spring vacation," Ellen said thoughtfully. "I've been thinking about it. Maybe to Barnard. Where I could be close to things in the theater—"

"Bubber, we'll just have to have Ellen meet Sissy," Courtney appealed to her husband. "Why don't we take her to see the play and then go backstage afterwards? You'll just adore Sissy, Ellen. She's the sweetest, most unspoiled—and I know she'll just be dying to meet you when she hears she has a cousin who wants to go on the stage too—"

"I'd love that—" Ellen said enthusiastically.

"Well, are you free tomorrow night?" Walter asked, then said, "Darn! We've got to go out to dinner with the Hardings tomorrow night, Suster."

Suster nodded sadly.

"Well, we'll make it during the spring vacation, Favorite Cuz," Walter promised heartily. "You write us when you're coming and we'll set it up. Maybe Ella can come along too, Suster, and we can have a real family reunion. And talk about all the ones not lucky enough to be present."

Ellen laughed and said that would be just fine, that she would be looking forward. They went to the living room for liqueurs and coffee, and after Ellen had finished her Chartreuse she noticed

Courtney stifling a yawn. "I'd better go. I've got a busy day tomorrow," Ellen said.

"Shopping?"

"Yes, more or less."

"More or less?" Walter asked in mock amazement. "I never heard of a woman shopping more or less!"

"All right, *more* then," Ellen laughed.

He went to the closet to get her coat, and to her surprise, returned wearing his, his hat in hand, ready to go out.

"Oh, you don't have to go with me!" she exclaimed. Her heartbeat told her how frightened she was.

"I don't *have* to do anything but die," he said in firm gallantry. "It's quite a piece from here back to your hotel."

"But I can go by myself! After all, I came up here by myself."

But Walter was insistent, and they argued about it pleasantly all the way down in the elevator. At last he consented to just put her in a cab.

The doorman hailed a taxi, and as it stopped in front of the house, Walter said quietly, "Now, look here, Cuz—no, don't stop me—you've got something bothering you. I knew you were in some sort of trouble as soon as you came in that door tonight, even though I don't know you too awfully well. Now, I don't want you to think you have to tell me what it is, but whatever it is, I never knew a trouble yet that couldn't be helped at least a little by some of this." He took her hand and handed her into the cab, pressing it to reassure her just before he released it. "Now, call us up when you get to the hotel," he said, "and let us know you outwitted the white slave boys." He slammed the cab door, giving the driver the address and handing him a bill to take care of the fare, and watched as the taxi drove away.

Ellen looked back, raised her gloved hand, the one Walter had held, to wave, and a check fell on the seat. She picked it up curiously, unfolded it, and by the light of the streetlamps which flashed by, she saw that it was drawn to the order of Ellen Tate Terrill Potts in the sum of $500.

# VIII

"Look," Gloria said persuasive, diplomatic, although she was getting tired of it, "this is no time to turn chicken."

"Chicken, that's what I had for dinner last night," Ellen murmured.

"Look, kid, I don't care what you had for dinner—or rather, I'm glad you did and hope you enjoyed it—but this is not the time to *quit*."

"I didn't say I was quitting," Ellen said dully. "I just said I didn't feel up to it today."

They were having breakfast in a cafeteria, only a few blocks from the Fifth Avenue stores. Gloria was on her second cup of black coffee, her hangover desiring nothing else, and Ellen was drawing her fork tines through the congealing, remains of an egg yolk, as she had been doing ever since just after she had announced she was going back to their West Side hotel and stay in bed all day. Gloria had been giving her a going over ever since.

"I wish to God Steve was here!" Gloria said vehemently.

"Lord! Leave me alone. You act like I'm a defecting member of your cell block in the Communist Party. I'll do as I please. And I'd tell Steve that too!"

"Like hell you would," Gloria said scornfully. "Anyway," she added, going back to an earlier subject, "I tell you I did not spend the night with him. I met this john—"

"I don't care, I don't care," Ellen said wearily. "I am not jealous. It has nothing to do with it. Just because I made some remark about your not coming back last night doesn't mean I'm mad at you both and therefore won't go out today. I just don't want to, that's all. I've got a feeling about it."

"Look here, kid," Gloria leaned closer, "everybody gets hunches about these things, but they usually don't work out. You're not going to get caught today any more than you did yesterday. Besides, Steve keeps telling me how smart you are, and a smart kid like you oughtn't to be superstitious."

Ellen gave her an impatient, derogatory little laugh. "It's not that, Gloria. Take my word for it. It's just that I can't face *anybody* today—all those awful crowds—"

"Believe me, sweetie, I did not sleep with Steve—"

Ellen gave her a poisoned look and removed her hand from under the one Gloria had pressed on hers for emphasis. Gloria looked glum.

"All right, I'll tell you," she said finally, looking Ellen straight in the face. "What I told you about Steve and me is perfectly true. I did meet a john—a guy, that is, a real—oh, some other time I'll tell you about that—I expect to be seeing a lot of him—but Steve met someone too—"

"Oh?" Ellen asked with interest.

"Not what you think—an old bag. She was in the same party with my fellow. They came into the place before we did, sat in the back, and I had them spotted when Steve got there—"

"Was the great Mr. McCoy late?"

"Yes," said Gloria hurriedly, not liking the interruption. "He was doing some of his writing. Anyways, we sat in the back too, so they could get a load of us like we did them. And just like it was mental telepathy or something the ones we had picked out of the bunch—this old gal and my fellow—well, they ditched the others and came back. And that's where Steve is, up there with her."

"How disgusting," said Ellen.

"Oh, she's not so bad. Quite a gal, got a real good sense of humor."

"She must have had to want to go into a place like The Raven Room. I suppose she and the others came down craving Village atmosphere?"

"Yeah. The others in their party were out-of-town buyers—get that—who wanted to see some freak shows. Johnny gave 'em all something to remember him by. Anyways, after they ditched the visitors and came back, we all sat around talking shop—the garment business, that's what both of them are in—isn't that a howl? So naturally, we all had a lot in common. Steve put it on thick; pretended his old man used to run a fancy dress shop in Toledo—"

"I can imagine," Ellen said drily.

"—Then nature sort of took its course—"

"Where did nature's course take Steve to?" Ellen asked, looking fairly angry now.

"I think the hag said West End Avenue. She's a Jew. My fellow is too."

"I always heard that Jews make the best husbands," Ellen said vacantly.

"Unfortunately mine already is one. I sure could go for him too," Gloria added wistfully.

Ellen frowned, and knew that her shoulders drooped; she didn't care. "I feel sick," she announced. "Really sick."

"Over Steve? Or maybe that chicken? Hotel food—especially chicken, even in the best—"

"Naturally, I mean Steve. Why would he go after an old one except for one reason—"

"What's wrong with that? She's a widow, lonesome, has lots of jack and is willing to pay for a little fun—"

Ellen gave a dismal sigh. "It just seems so horrible."

"You're not hardboiled enough, kid. Steve's got ambition. Real what they call drive. And he's willing to do anything he has to to get there. Supposing this old dame set him up, gave him a nice apartment where he could write all day on his book, plenty of dough, would you blame him for it?"

"And what would he do all night?"

"Ahhh," Gloria made a face, dismissing the seriousness of this. "Those old gals—when they get to be that age, they don't want it so much. Probably not more than once or twice a month. What they want is to have somebody young and attractive and funny around for company. She wouldn't bother him much. He'd probably spend most of his evenings with us—with you, that is."

"I'm not so sure," Ellen said.

"Oh, yes, he would, hon. Steve thinks the world of you. He wouldn't walk out on you."

Ellen made no reply, or bother to correct Gloria's interpretation of what she had said; she knew she didn't mean it really anyway. It was just said impulsively, out of hurt. She was still Steve's. Anytime.

"Forgive him?" Gloria inquired, searching Ellen's quiet somber face.

"What else can I do?"

"Sure, kid. He goes for you. You know that. By the way," she said, her voice bright with relief, "did you cry yourself to sleep last night?"

"No, and I didn't write any of those dear Mom letters Steve is so certain I'm going to dash off when his back is turned. I told him I just write them to get them off my chest every now and then. I wouldn't mail them."

"Well, where does your family think you are?" Gloria asked cautiously, glad that Ellen had brought the subject up herself, for she was very curious to know.

"Well, after that telegram I sent when we first got here I called them up, and said I was fine, and having a good time and was on my way back to Chicago."

Gloria looked dumbfounded. "Chicago? Suppose they write to you there?"

"Suppose they do? I almost never wrote home anyway. I call them once in a while. They don't know whether the call is coming from New York or Timbuctoo. I always call station-to-station and tell the operator not to say where it's coming from, just in case."

"Well, I'll be! You are a sly boots!" Gloria declared with feeling. Then she frowned. "Wait a minute. Didn't you tell Steve they were mad at you and had cut off your money? How do they think you're getting by?"

"That's simple," Ellen shrugged casually. "My tuition was paid, my room and board was all paid for the year, lab fees and everything. And they think I'm just being too proud to ask for money. They figure I had some saved—my allowance was really a lot more than I needed, you know—or they think I'm borrowing it. We don't discuss it."

"Funny folks you've got," Gloria shook her head incredulously. "But what about the school. Won't they write your folks that you've dropped out?"

Ellen shook her head. "Why? I formally resigned before I left, got my credits and everything."

"Jee-sus Christ!"

"And furthermore, I gave my forwarding address in care of a girl I knew at Sweet Briar. So all my mail goes to her. She knows all about it—all about Steve, that is. Thinks it's very romantic. I told her I'd write and let her know when the wedding was to be and that she could come up and be my bridesmaid—and bring all my mail with her then. She's still waiting, but I'll write to her soon."

Gloria studied her, a worried expression on her face. "You aren't that serious about Steve, are you, kid?"

"I guess I was. I'm not anymore. He was different in Chicago. When he thought I was Miss Rich-bitch. On his good behavior, I guess. No, I don't kid myself about marrying Steve anymore. Besides, it's probably too late for that."

Gloria scrutinized her carefully, and decided it was better not to ask her what she meant about that "too late" business; the kid looked worked up enough.

Artificially brightening, Gloria said in an enthusiastic voice. "Me, I never thought I'd get hung up on this love kick until I met this fellow last night—now, I don't know. I could sure go for him. I'd like for you to meet him. He's somebody I think you'd think was a real gentleman. He's been to college too. Very elegant fellow. Went to Harvard."

"Rich, I trust," Ellen said rather tonelessly, just to be cooperative.

"Boy, is he ever wealthy! He had a wad on him as big around as my wrist. And he's generous. You know what he did? Look here," she reached in her purse and proudly disclosed a $100 bill.

"Not bad," Ellen said feigning admiration.

"Not bad? Well just look here at this, if you think that's something. This he gave me because—well the $100 was what he thought I should get—but this, he said, was just for me. He said the minute he saw me just something about the look in my eyes told him I was in deep, deep trouble. But that I didn't have to talk about it. But that this might take the trouble out of my eyes, or help take it out." Slyly, triumphantly, she produced four new crisp $100 bills.

Ellen stared for a moment, then threw her head back and howled with laughter.

## IX

Gloria hurried Ellen out to the street, and was ready to slap her face to drive out the hysteria, when suddenly Ellen stopped.

"What the hell was that for?" Gloria asked angrily.

"Relief."

"Relief from what? If you think I'm going to throw this five hundred bucks into the partnership pot, you're crazy. I've got plenty of uses for this $500, and they all have to do with me."

"I didn't mean that," Ellen said lamely. "I meant I was relieved because things seem to be looking up—you found this john, and Steve may have landed a cushy deal, so maybe we can all quit this racket sooner than we thought."

"Yes," Gloria agreed, but said in some concern, "but we won't leave you high and dry."

Ellen shrugged. "Don't worry about me. Something will work out."

"You'll, strike it lucky too," Gloria said with cheer, but doubtful conviction.

"Yes, things will work out," Ellen repeated. "Now, come on. Where're we going today?"

Gloria looked at her mystified. "I thought you were the one who wanted to chicken out."

"I've changed my mind. I feel better."

"Hearing about my five hundred bucks did it, huh? But don't tell Steve about it—"

"I wouldn't dream of it. But Gloria, getting all that money just like, well, almost like finding it—didn't it make you think about cutting out and going off, not taking any more things from stores—?"

"Are *you* crazy? Honey, nobody ever got rich spending money, you get rich making it."

"Okay, that answers my question. Come on."

They walked down Fifth Avenue, melding with the crowd, looking like two expensive, pampered, young wives whose sole purpose in life was to dispose of their husbands' money. They turned into the large department store Steve had selected for this day's morning operation. They walked along the aisles, chatting together, laughing frequently, as if they were as intent on gossiping as they were on shopping. It was a store they had been in once before, so they knew the routine, and they felt as casual as they looked. They had their equipment: a shopping bag bearing the store's label, and containing a few odds and ends.

They paused now and again at a counter and fingered the gloves or scarves or whatever with open disdain, and when a hovering clerk, obviously new, asked if she could help them, Gloria's "No thanks!" was imperious, scornful and perfect. They made their way to the sweater department, for they had arranged to concentrate on the fur-trimmed cashmeres meant for semi-formal wear. The prices started at just under a hundred and went up.

"Darling, isn't this adorable!" Ellen cried suddenly to her friend, and snatched up a little lambs' wool sleeveless sweater as if it had been hers all the time. "Wouldn't it be perfect for Hobe Sound?"

"How much?" Gloria asked in the beady-eyed voice appropriate to the bargain hunter who could buy and sell the store.

Ellen examined the price tag. "Sweet-tee!" she exclaimed. "It's $10.95!"

"It's been marked down, Madame," said a clerk at her elbow. She beamed rather wistfully at both of them.

Gloria, not giving this person or her existence the slightest glance, took the sweater authoritatively from her friend's hand. "Too small for you," she said flatly.

"It is not!" Ellen protested.

"We have it in other sizes, Madam. Other colors too. What size does Madame wear?"

"This is my size," Ellen said crisply. "I'll take it."

Gloria glowered in pretended disapproval. "I thought you wanted to exchange that cashmere," she said stiffly. "Charge or cash?" asked the saleswoman.

"Charge," Ellen said, as if the transaction had begun to bore her now that the excitement of selection was over.

"You'd better not," Gloria hissed in a very voluble undertone. "Remember what you told me about Philip's seeing last month's?"

Quickly, then, Ellen amended her instruction. "I think I'll pay cash after all. Here. Don't bother to wrap it. I'll just pop it in here with the rest of this junk." She tried to take the sweater from the clerk and tuck it away in her shopping bag.

"But Madam, I have to write up the sale and give you a ticket—otherwise—hah, hah," said the clerk nervously, "if someone stopped you and you had no sales slip…"

"Oh, bother the sales slip! I throw 'em away the minute I get them, and if someone wants to think I swiped it, that's just too bad. Just give me the sweater and my change."

"But if you want to return it, not having the sales slip—"

"Really," Ellen said with just a touch of haughty exasperation, "if a store doesn't know its own merchandise—"

Nonetheless, the saleswoman dutifully tore off the detachable corner of the price tag, rang up the sale, and handed Ellen the receipt, which Ellen simply dropped on the floor. Then she and Gloria, looking very spoiled and smug, marched away.

The clerk looked after them, still smiling her good-natured

wistful smile.

They went up to the fur department on the ninth floor and tried on minks to kill time, keeping up their dialogue, embroidering their fiction with happy abandon.

Then they returned to the sweaters. While Gloria stalked over to the counter where Ellen had made the purchase, Ellen carefully went through the cashmeres, tossing them about as if they were rags. This one and that she held up to her, for size, or held at arm's length to appraise, squinting at the workmanship, making faces, wearing that absorbed look of one about to talk aloud to one's self.

While this was going on, Gloria was bedeviling the saleswoman. She was demanding that the woman fit her in a sweater exactly like her friend's. Nothing suited her, however. She complained that it was too large or too small, or when the size was satisfactory, she said that the cooler was off—all this accompanied by frequent requests to Ellen to "come look at this, darling. Let's see if the color is the same as yours," etc.

"In a minute," Ellen replied absently. "I want to see if there are any left here that might do." By this time she had the most expensive sweater on the counter selected, and in the bag. Listlessly, as if she had given up the hope that she might find something she liked, she strolled over to Gloria. "Now what is it?" she asked. "Hurry up, I'm starved."

"Is this the same color as yours?"

"Let's see what you've got in the bag."

"What?" asked Ellen, and then she saw that they had been quietly joined by a woman in a rather ratty mink coat, wearing a hat that was sufficiently hideous and costly to make her indistinguishable from a thousand other women who passed in and out of the store daily. She was, in short, the store detective.

"Come on, Miss," the woman said brusquely. "Open up that bag. I saw you slip that cashmere in there."

"You can be sued for this," Gloria said sternly.

"Come on, come on, the only ones who ever talk like that are the ones who haven't got a case," she said. "Come on, now," she made a grab for the shopping bag. "I was watching you. While your friend here got the clerk's attention. Oh, I've had my eye on you quite a while."

"You impertinent, common—" Ellen said, but her voice shook.

Gloria's face was tense, and her fright showed in her eyes, but her voice was poised. "Take your hands off my friend. *I* know the law. My husband's a lawyer. I know you can be sued for every dime this store is worth for trying to apprehend a suspect while she's still on the premises."

"You don't know anything," the detective told her sourly.

Ellen's hand trembled badly as they all watched her rummage in the shopping bag. She brought out the sweater, and the detective grabbed it out of her hands. She turned it over carefully, not looking so sure of herself anymore.

Gloria held her breath. Then she saw: while the argument had been going on somehow, miraculously, Ellen had managed to tear off the proper corner of the price tag, so it was a genuine sale!

"The sales slip," the detective ordered. She reached out her hand to Ellen, and even snapped her fingers. "Come on, come on. Where's the sales slip?"

"I don't have it," Ellen said unfalteringly. "I don't keep them."

The detective made a sibilant noise. of disbelief and impatience. "Okay, miss, if you want it that way. I saw you put that sweater in that shopping bag. We'll just go upstairs to the office and you can tell them your story."

"All right, so you saw me," Ellen said hotly. "So what? I think I have a right to remove my own sweater from a shopping bag and then put it back in again!"

"What were you removing it for? Trying to make a little private exchange—maybe two for one?"

"You horrid creature!" Ellen blazed. "As a matter of fact, I was planning to exchange it. That's why we ever came in this awful store today. I was just comparing it with some of the others to see if there was anything better."

The detective didn't turn a hair. "All right, miss, you just go tell that upstairs." She put a strong hand on Ellen's arm to lead her off.

"I beg your pardon," said a tiny, timid voice, "but I overheard Madam earlier when she bought a lambs' wool and Madam mentioned something about exchanging a cashmere." The clerk had spoken, and now her eyes, wide with fright at what she had done, looked from one to the other of the three, begging them like a dumb animal. And like a dumb animal she hardly knew what she begged for. She simply wanted them to take away her fright.

All the same, the detective released Ellen's arm reluctantly. "I still don't believe it," she said, surly as ever. "You're a thief and I know it. You think you're clever."

"I'm clever enough to close out my charge account here forever!" Ellen raged, her voice high and indignant.

"Just you do that," said the woman. "Or maybe I can save you the bother. Just hand over your charge-a-plate and I'll take care of the matter for you."

"Go to hell!" Ellen shouted at her, and with quick, angry strides, heads up, she and Gloria marched out of the store, looking from neither side to side at the women who had heard the argument from a distance and were curious as to what it had all been about.

X

Stephen, propped up in a broad Hollywood bed, his warm nakedness sheathed in a wine-colored satin eiderdown, intensified his hold on the ruby-red telephone into which he was listening. At the same time the casual pace at which his eyes had been roving critically through the unfamiliar but not cheap furnishings and objects of the room changed into swift birdlike flight, his eyes perching briefly on this and that, only to flit off again. He was now entirely speechless with consternation, and could no longer summon the bored grunt of "yeah, yeah. Go on," which he had injected into Gloria's conversation when she first began to tell him about it. He listened fully now; his mental hold as tight on the words as his hand on the telephone. And his quick flitting glances around the room, delivered through narrowed eyes, were like tiny express conveyances for his thoughts. What Gloria was saying was serious; something had to be done.

At last he spoke. "I'll call you tonight. Keep her in the hotel until I do. No, I can't get away any sooner." And he hung up angrily, the way a busy executive hangs up on a secretary who has delivered an adverse piece of business news.

He lowered himself carefully back into supine place on the bed, not so much as if he were an invalid trying to protect himself from pain, but indolently, and as if he handled precious merchandise. Once settled, his indolence continued, even to the luxury of putting his hands behind his head, arms akimbo, lolling like a bathing beauty. But he did his best thinking when he was entirely com-

fortable, and except for the unexpected annoyance of the news received during his routine call to Gloria, he was entirely comfortable.

And was the news so shattering after all? Wasn't Ellen always
more or less hysterical? Actually, the quality of—fright? resentment?—well, unfriendliness in Gloria's voice had been the factor
which momentarily sent him into ramrod alertness. She had made
it sound as if it were his fault that Ellen had nearly been caught
with the sweater, and as if it were his personal obligation to come
kiss Ellen's tears away and smooth her fevered brow. God damn
them! With a scowl so mighty that it was worthy of an Olympian,
he leaped from the bed, viciously consigning the coverlet to the
floor where it lay in a dejected red silky pool, and strode about the
room as if he were an impassioned actor at a dress rehearsal.

The ludicrousness of his behavior brought his steps to a sudden halt, and he laughed to himself, looking down at his own nakedness. How absurd and pathetic for a naked man to ever lose his
temper! He hopped back into bed, springy and lighthearted as a
young pup, and lay there grinning.

He put his hands behind his head again, and crossed his well-
made athletic legs, not too hairless to be unmanly, or too hirsute
to be unsightly, but just right. He pointed his big toe at the crystal
chandelier in the "widow woman's" bedroom ceiling. Ornate
enough for a ball room. What a vulgar, comfortable old cow she
was! And he inwardly beamed with pleasure at things past-and
those to come. Mrs. Silverman just suited him at the present.
Theirs would be the most pleasant of arrangements. Who would
ever have thought that he, Steve McCoy, could have touched—
and all over—an old doll like that, no matter what the price? Why,
he had even liked it! He thought of the huge breasts, big as picture
hats and as floppy, and he found himself lovingly fondling them in
memory. If this was an unexpected mother complex coming out,

she could have his gold star anytime.

As he reminisced about the night before, his heart melting with the ease of an eye watering from sentiment, he heard footsteps nearing the bedroom door. Quickly, he righted himself, putting away Gratitude, Kindliness, Interest, Relief, and Speculation as if they were a set of child's blocks with which he had been cluttering the place, and once more got out of bed. He performed two full circles of striding, Indian-fashion, in the middle of the floor, as if it were some ritual to insure good luck, and met her at the door. She stepped in and his strong arms went around her lovingly, possessively, holding her in an embrace so perfect for the occasion and the person that it seemed calculated not only to restore her lost youth but make her know that truly the best had come last. And Stephen, who actually disliked the act of kissing even in the height of ardor, considering it an unnecessary bit of interpersonal nastiness, like swapping chewing gum, administered to Mrs. Silverman's lips a kiss of everlasting radiance and honesty, a glad kiss, simple as a child's, yet deep and satisfying as a man's kiss should be. She was overwhelmed.

"Not since Hymie," she breathed, looking up at him like a smitten young girl.

"Go on, Essie. He wasn't all that good."

"He was a man, my Hymie," she said gravely, and holding him away momentarily from her portly, heaving bosom took a serious and beseeching look at him. "I shouldn't insult the dead, God forbid, but I'll tell you something Steve—" She broke off to study his face again, his sly grin and the twinkle in his eye, then continued in her slightly accented English, calling him by name again, pronouncing it so that it seemed to be spelled "Stiv"—"If my Hymie were alive today and he and I should have went to Greenwich Village so the buyers should see some artists and go home so they should say they had a big time in New York and saw the town—"

"And if you should have met me? Like last night?" he suggested not untenderly.

She nodded, her eyes shy with shame and love.

"Gorgeous Essie!" he cried by way of reward and tried to swoop her up as if she weighed a hundred pounds less. She cooperated by grabbing him to her rather fiercely and they led each other off to bed.

Essie, some four hours before, had fully clothed herself for the day, and now, struggling out of her corseted business self into her hubris bedroom self, proved to be both laborious and unamorous. Steve watched her haste and frustrations from the bed, lying on his side, his head propped up on an elbow on the coverlet like a god observing mortality from a cloud. But her movements did not disgust him, for which he was grateful and secretly surprised. On the other hand, however, he did not feel involved in any way, and it did not occur to him to spontaneously bound out of bed, as he would have done had Esther Silverman been a young and lovely woman, or obliged to from a sense of gallantry had she been just a young one, and devoutly assist her, his touch intimate and lingering as he unhitched stubborn garments, freeing flesh to his contact. Instead, he lay and watched; not unlustful, not uneager, but bemused.

Exasperated and inflamed from work rather than passion, Esther turned to him when she was nearly undressed and remarked that she was the one who "should have stood in bed."

Steve enjoyed this very much, and when she came to him a moment later, undressed at last and lumbering rather heavily and certainly panting, he held his arms out to her open wide. She fell into them like a gazelle and he made love to her manfully, and as if his heart was really in it.

However, this aspect of their togetherness having been accomplished, followed by the verbal summary period of quietly spoken, whispered if not hushed exchanges about their feelings for each other, the degrees of satisfaction each had obtained, the time for Reality rolled in.

Esther, whose turn it now was to prop herself up on an elbow and gaze at him, did so, her look as impersonal and relaxed as though they were merely out somewhere having cocktails together. "So, Stevie, if I should give you this money so you should write this book—"

"It's mostly written, Essie," he said quietly, patiently, having told her all about it before.

"But if I should give you this money—" her voice trailed off, weighted down by tentativeness.

Steve sat up energetically and again, seeing the need for it, went into his song and dance. "You won't be giving it to me, Essie—"

"I know," she said meaningfully. "Giving, I will not be—"

"Don't start that 'you're buying me' stuff again either," he interrupted to say. "Sure, I can go out and lay a couple of dozen dolls a couple of dozen years younger if I wanted to. Don't get sex mixed up with business. I like you. You like me. I'd like to lay you whether you were the head of a big dress business on Seventh Avenue or a clerk in the dime store—"

"Stevie, calm yourself. Who's arguing?"

"But I want you to believe me, Essie. This money will be just to help me until I get an advance on the book and get on my feet—"

"Tell me something, Stevie. Your papa, did he ever have a store out West?"

"No," said Steve. "That was a lie. A gag."

"A come-on?"

"Sure." He gave her a broad grin and she gave him one right back. They understood each other.

They talked briefly some more as they dressed—Steve said he had to hurry, had to meet a guy in the Village and she said she understood—and made more detailed plans. With the money she would presently give him, he would, he said, pay back the money he had told her about the night before, that this guy was hounding him for, would get his typewriter and some other things out of hock, and would move into a suite at the Sydney Hotel, one they had agreed upon as a convenient and inexpensive location in mid-town. He would also open a bank account and show her his bank book so she could see the amount he deposited was what he said; that all this was on the up and up.

They went into the wide, sunny living room and Essie asked him if he'd like a drink, or would he like breakfast or lunch.

"I'll take the drink," he said, twinkling his eyes at her. His joy was as undisguised as a child's.

He followed her over to the bar, well stocked and well made. Not what he would have chosen as a piece of furniture for his own living room, but like Essie, comfortable, expansive and "the best" in its class.

He admired her broad back and ample strong arms; also her behind. She was a woman who had taken middle age quietly, and with a certain resigned charm usually found in the slight and the young and the sensitive.

"I'll bet you were a knockout when you were twenty, baby," he told her.

"I was a cute little chippy," she said smiling. He wondered if she knew what chippy meant and decided she didn't. "I was slim. Like your girlfriend. Not so pretty in the face."

"Here, let me see your profile." Steve said and turned her head so he could see it. "I admire it," he said.

"Keep your words for your book," she said.

"You're a real gal, baby."

She shrugged, using all of the upper part of her body, but she was obviously pleased. "I've got no time for books," she told him as she settled herself on the wide, plump couch which complemented her own frame. "But yours I'll take time for."

He beamed, but again he hoped she would not ask him to tell her about it as she had last night. "I'll talk it away," he had told her then, using the novelist's first prerogative. But it wasn't just that. If Essie ever did read his book she would see too much. She would know just how autobiographical it was. This set him to less pleasant thoughts, concerning Ellen, Gloria, the whole now almost repugnant operation which because of Essie he would be free in a few blessed moments to kick in the teeth if he so desired, or kick in the ass where it belonged.

"You frown like Hymie even," she said. "You must be worried again."

"I am," he admitted. "But, Essie, not like before. You're saving my life, baby."

"Life," she said, again with a shrug. "What is it? Like money, you got it or you don't. Both, you got to work for."

Stephen agreed and stood up.

Essie stood up too, her silk-shod bottom unrealistically spherical and smooth instead of lumpy and sagging as it was without the girdle she once again wore. Stephen felt no desire to even try to pinch such a fortress though he felt perhaps some such gesture was required. He tilted back her face which was easier, and which he even liked doing. "You're my gal," he told her.

Her answering smile was solely on her lips. The eyes were undeceived. She put an envelope into his hand. It was a very fat one and bore the name of her firm; it was, in fact, a pay envelope used for giving her employees their salaries in cash. But it was his own fault; he had requested cash.

He did not kiss her at the door, and she made no effort to kiss him, nor was there any signal from her eyes that such an endearment was expected. Instead, she looked sure of him.

"Good-bye, baby," he said.

"Good-bye, Steve," she answered, and closed the door even before he reached the elevator. No reaffirmation had been necessary for their date tomorrow night.

XI

Though Steve considered it unwise to count money in a taxi-cab, this time he couldn't resist it. Two thousand free bucks, not stolen but given!

He broke open the seal of the envelope as the taxi speeded him downtown toward the bar around the comer from the West Side hotel where Gloria and Ellen had their permanent quarters; he planned to phone from there—not to tell them about the loot he had gotten from the widow woman, but to see what the hell they were so out of their wigs over. Anybody could "almost" get caught; almost and getting were two different things.

He withdrew the fat wad of bills. A hundred dollar bill was, of course, on top. But to his amazement, as he rifled the collection, the denominations changed. They got smaller and smaller. Instead of the twenty 100s he had expected to find, or a few hundreds and a lot of fifties, or maybe even a five hundred note, he found chicken feed—tens and twenties. He counted it through. Five hundred dollars. He must be wrong. He counted it again. "Five hundred God damn lousy dollars," he exclaimed aloud.

"Yeah, everything's going up," agreed the driver.

Steve heard this geniality, knew the moment for the ironical thing it was—a sort of literary bijou—but took it as indifferently as a martyr receiving his hundredth stone. He knew there would be more. Yes indeed there would be more. More stones and more money. The smart old bitch. What a sweet trusting fool he had been to think she was a sweet trusting fool. Now, she was assured that he would be back; she had more than just his word for it.

He played with the packet of money as a gambler toys in his spare time with a deck of cards. What now? Fuck the girls!

"Take me to the White Horse!" he commanded the driver.

"What say, buddy?"

"The White Horse Bar!" he rasped and gave him the address in a voice of precise and imperious exasperation. "In *Green Which Village*," he added sarcastically.

The driver paid this no heed. Steve settled back for the long ride. He wished for the homburg to push back from his head; he longed to unbuckle his belt, unzip his fly, loosen his collar, and relax into indigestion as if after a long and ghastly meal. Thinking about Essie Silverman now made him good and sick, and thinking about Gloria and Ellen was like remembering creampuffs and sauerkraut after one has vomited. God damn women. And his manuscript lay cold and lonely in his luggage in some locker in Grand Central Station. Truly deserted. He sat up and looked at his money again. At least it was five hundred found bucks. He could still check into the hotel and quit the racket, if he wanted. After all, that pawnshop business and the pressing loan had been a lot of crap. But he had wanted that bank account. Now the roll would simply stay in his pocket.

Five hundred bucks. Lay her twice a month for that. No more. She had cheated him. She had virtually stolen from him. Look at the morning he had wasted while she went to her "business," as she called it, to get the cash! He shook his head from side to side. He wanted to get drunk.

With this conviction in mind, he strode into the White Horse and set about realizing his resolution with boilermakers.

After the third round, a lot of things were clear: he'd give Madam Turkey Wattles two quick ones—and none for the road— then get another five Cs or nothing. He'd lay her and it on the same line. Meantime, of course, there was no thought of abandoning the racket with the kids, except for the hotel part. He would go ahead and move into the Sydney, as planned, rent himself a typewriter so that the work would go faster, and never leave the joint except to make returns to the stores, eat, and do his duty by the old bag until the book was finished. The girls in the evenings could do whatever they liked; their days were numbered. Of course they could visit him now and again, separately or together; preferably the latter which he found more stimulating if not exciting. He sat there thinking about it, his head bowed over his drink, not looking up or caring to except to reorder. The bar, however, was almost empty as it usually was at this time of day and he would have found it dull if his interests had been at that moment outwardly directed.

At last he seemed to sense this, as though the quiet and emptiness had registered on his skin, and instinctively he got up, paid his check, and went out to move toward something more lively and lighter, but still as unconscious as a moth.

He cut through the West Village, bound for the central part, by way of Bank Street, feeling not at all unsteady on his feet, but a little light in the head from the drinks—but far from the state he wanted. It occurred to him that he should call the girls, but the thought was fleeting and furry, a sense of duty rather than a desire. As master it was important to keep them in thrall, keep strong discipline as lord of the manor. But where did the expression "drunk as a lord" come from if not from such flights of negligence?

At one point he stopped to blow his nose, looking around the prim residential street as if to see that he was entirely alone, and blowing the nose was therefore proper. That was when he saw the bookshop. It was directly across from where he stood; obviously new—he could tell by the lettering on the window and the paint— and the kind of shop that was sure to be chi-chi avant garde, not beatnik: it would have a progressive lady proprietor or a fairy-type running it; in summer it would have an awning—not green-and-white striped, but pearl gray, or violet with black-edged scallops, or whatever color was good with Bergdorf's this year. And the merchandise? Yes, it would be the kind of book emporium which would of course stock his book when it was published. He crossed the street.

He stood outside for a bit and studied the titles. All the Zen Buddhist crap. The new issue of TEXAS QUARTERLY with the Katherine Anne Porter novel-in-progress excerpt. A copy of BOR-STAL BOY, TRY OR ELEQANCE; all of—or what looked like all of—Lawrence Durrell, which meant they were an out-of-print place as well as current in-print booksellers. Then he went in. He wandered toward the paperbacks, saw that they were as "selected" as he had expected them to be, and turned to go out.

"Hi, Larry," someone said.

Larry had never been one of Steve's names, but he looked around anyway. He saw that the girl at the desk—and she was a girl in every sense of the word—was engaged in conversation with a pencil-thin youth, complete with a beard as thin as the growth at the timberline, and blue jeans seemingly even thinner than himself. His fragility was crammed into them, and bulging at the places where he could bulge. Larry, Steve surmised to himself and continued toward the door.

"At least you can say good-bye if you can't say hello," called the girl again. He stopped.

"I beg your pardon," he said. "Me?"

He stared at her while she stared at him. "Oh, but you're *not* Larry," she said with a mouth as rich and red as a candy fruit drop.

"Not even a little," he said, deliberately beguiling, for this girl was some dish. "I'm Stephen McCoy," he added.

"The real McCoy," she cried in a delight which made him wince, pained for her youth, pained for her unoriginality.

"What is reality?" asked the blue-jeaned young man in a stagey voice that was tiresomely airy. "I mean, really?"

But Steve didn't even glance in his direction; once had been enough. Instead he looked at the girl behind the desk. Her hair was as heavy and black as a thicket, eyes the color of a blackbird's wing and almost pupilless with their density. Hair and eyes, he decided, would remain eternal enigmas for all who looked upon her; this part of her was impenetrable, but not so the mouth, the nose, the merry curve of her rather dark-skinned face. She was a beauty.

"I'm Apple Ashby," she said to stop his staring and her own.

"Not really," he purred.

And later when the pencil-thin youth, having gotten the point that there was no point, that there was no part for him in this bedroom comedy, had withdrawn as silently as an extra fading into the wings, Apple and Steve headed back to the White Horse. She peremptorily shut the shop, saying there was no business anyway.

On the way there, they first of all held hands; then he told her her name wasn't Apple and she admitted it gaily, shriekingly, in fact, as excited as a child on his first ferris wheel ride. She was ecstatic at being proved a fraud, and, in turn, tried to provide Steve with the same pleasure.

"But my name *is* McCoy," he insisted. "I was christened Stephen Xavier McCoy."

"You're *Jewish*," she cried at him, "not Irish. Don't tell me."

"No, Apple-baum, balm of my present-day heart, I am Irish," he replied expansively, realizing he was having quite a good time.

She said she couldn't believe it. He offered to prove it. She said it was not wise to sleep with strangers, even attractive, bright and witty ones.

He then caught her in his arms, holding her to him as if she were a harmless but elusive wild animal, and kissed her hair, eschewing her lips. But she sought his, gave him a biting kiss. They broke away, their separation leaving a slight sucking sound behind like two joined vacuums suddenly confronted with air. They continued to the White Horse.

Stephen watched the way her mane tossed around in the cold winter wind and was reminded of Ellen's pale birchy silken hair—for some reason—which was picked up in strands when the wind blew, as if nature was carding it. Apple, seeing the look on his face, wanted to know if he wrote poetry. He said he did. In a way it was not a lie. He expected her to squeeze his hand appreciatively at this, but since she didn't he squeezed hers.

They continued on to the White Horse in the sort of daze that was really a suspension: all things of consequence were underneath them, flowing like water, as if they traversed a high bridge, a bridge leading to the other side where there was nothing but one endless huge bed.

At the White Horse, they were vaguely aware that the sun was going down outside and that inside wonderful, mellowing boiler-makers were being quaffed and paid for by the drink; they might be ready to leave at any time.

"Do you want to come back with me to my hotel?" he asked her huskily.

"I don't have my diaphragm," she said, sounding a little whiney like Ellen.

"Where is it?"

She laughed at this. "At home on a shelf in the medicine cabinet. Where did you think it was? In my roommate?"

"Do you have one?" he inquired.

She shook her head. "Hate roommates, but I'm a lesbian." She gave him a square look, marred by her drunkenness, to see if he believed her.

"Come on. Let's go to your house."

"I'm a lesbian," she repeated.

"So am I," he said, tugging her from her bar stool.

"I hardly know you," she said as breathless and fresh as the apple she was supposed to be.

"So you said earlier. Come on, time to get acquainted."

She said she didn't believe so, and firmly resisted the tugging.

Without a word, Stephen dropped her hand, turned his back, and went out the door.

"Wait!" she cried after him and quickly scrambled off the bar stool.

By the time she caught up with him, he was almost to 14th Street; she caught at his arm, exhausted from the chase, unable to speak. "Stephen," she gasped.

Coldly he disengaged her hand and strode on.

"Stephen, *please*," she begged, stopping in the middle of the sidewalk, barring his way.

He stepped around her.

"Come on," she coaxed. "Let's go to my apartment."

He continued walking.

"Where are you going?" she asked.

"Uptown."

"May I come with you?"

"What for?"

"You know what for."

"No."

"Why not, Stephen?"

"I'm not in the mood."

"Good-bye then," she said rather wanly, and came to a hesitant stop.

"Good-bye. Perhaps some other time."

The faltering look of bewilderment on her white face seemed to please him. "Good-bye," he said again, squeezing her hand and giving her a coruscating smile.

## XII

"Undress me," said Stephen, rolling his eyes suggestively at Gloria. He lay full length on the lumpy double bed which came with the other questionable furnishings of his new suite at the Sydney. He was "trying it out," he had said to Gloria, who knew better, as he indolently unleashed his body, legs crossed at the ankles, hands behind his head, arms akimbo. His favorite position, and one he always took presexually when Gloria was lined up in his sights. It amused him to have her professional ministrations.

"Oh, Steve," she said tentatively, staying where she was. "Don't you ever get enough?" She was referring to his athletic (as he had described it) evening with Mrs. Silverman.

"You know better than that, baby," he said broadly and twisted a little in anticipated pleasure, for he knew Gloria would do as he asked. The little gambol with Apple Ashby had only satisfied his soul, leaving his aroused sexual appetite unslaked.

Gloria, however, still hesitated, thinking strongly of her new john. "We can't. Ellen will be here any minute."

"All the better," said Steve cheerfully, "She can join us."

"Not me she can't," Gloria said firmly. "You know she don't like a daisy chain."

"Frig her!" said Stephen and made a grab at Gloria who complied without further argument.

She undressed Steve with methodical skill but no enthusiasm. "Get with it, baby," he complained, displeased at her lack of warmth. "You aren't getting paid for this, you know." "Neither are you," she giggled, and quickly shed her own clothes and crawled in beside him.

His eyes were filmy and languorous with desire as he lay look-ing at her long, rosy body. "You look like a Modigliani nude," he said thickly and ran his hand along the line of her thigh. Then he cupped one of her ample, firm breasts and a sigh of ecstasy flut-tered from his lips; he lay back again, greatly excited but as passive as a woman, for Gloria to go about her business. This she did swiftly and unspeakingly, hoping to God that Steve wouldn't ask for the usual. But he did.

"Tell me about your john last night," he whispered. "Was he good? Come on, tell me about it."

Telling him about it ordinarily consisted in acting out, as they went along, all the phases of love-making which had passed be-tween Gloria and some john or other, picked at random from her experience, who had proved himself particularly noteworthy. But she did not feel like sharing her night with Victor Rose, and when Steve insisted, his whispering becoming faster and faster with ex-citement, she pulled a switch on him and recounted an amorous adventure she hadn't thought of in years. It seemed to satisfy him, and after describing various positions taken, the number of times the john had been aroused and fulfilled, the size of his sexual mem-ber, Stephen at last managed his own crisis, and fell away from her damp and exhausted.

"That was a good one," he panted, thinking he spoke for both of them. But this was not the case; he had left Gloria cold and a little disgusted. The contrast between the warm passion of Victor and the engineered excitation of cold Stephen made her wonder about the whole nature of love-making. She looked at him lying on the bed. Now she knew what the books meant when they said somebody looked spent. Steve looked not just spent but over-drawn. Every ounce of his spontaneous sexuality must have gone years ago, and now he could only get his kicks from the bizarre or artificial. It was really just masturbation. Thinking how far out he was, she said, "Steve, do you ever go in for the Mama and Papa business?"

He gave her a cruel smile. "Is that what your john really liked?" he asked, then added, "Never mind. But to answer your question, since it seems to have slipped your mind, that's the only way Ellen and I have ever done it. Now isn't that sweet?"

Gloria, who had witnessed the sexual act between Steve and Ellen on several occasions, felt properly chastised for not remembering. "I just thought Ellen was inhibited in front of me," she murmured.

"She is, baby!" Steve cried joyfully and leaped from the bed, refreshed now and restored. And not a minute too soon either, for Ellen was ringing the bell as they walked into the living room. He paused to knot his tie before he let her in.

Ellen looked from one to the other as she came in, but saw no telltale sign to confirm her suspicions, so sat down meekly while Stephen strutted around, showing off his shabby suite to her, eliciting her admiration of it as he had similarly elicited Gloria's earlier.

Being Stephen, he had capriciously scrapped his plan to keep mum about his "inheritance from the Widow Silverman." Instead he was boastful and boring; the beam of pleasure on his face was so broad that it was almost obscene in its self-satisfaction. "Yes, Stephen. It's wonderful," she murmured laconically as she had quite a number of times during his performance—this one in allusion to his new Royal portable which he had jumped up to look at for the third time. She wondered if he had talked over the department store scare with Gloria before she came; she wondered where he had been all day and if Gloria knew; she wondered when if ever he would cease all this wonderment with himself.

"What made you decide to make this hotel your permanent headquarters?" Ellen asked and waited for him to answer. Then she saw that he wasn't going to bother to answer. It infuriated her suddenly, and she got up and strolled to the window to quiet herself. It looked down eleven stories to the busy honeycomb that was Times Square. She gazed out on the scene which had become a snowscape, only the snow, the first of the season, was not the sticking kind. It was the lubricating variety which seemed to oil and polish the streets, heightening the explosive flashes of color which came from the neon lights. It was just Stephen's sort of view, vulgar, bright, busy. Ellen dropped the cheap material of the curtain with a finality which perfectly expressed her mood, her washed-out feeling and abysmal disgust. But she didn't turn back to Stephen and Gloria. Instead she stood staring unseeingly at the curtain. It was made of some crazy material, and reminded her exactly of her own mind: thin, blank and soiled.

"What's the time?" Gloria asked her, for having inspected Stephen's lookout earlier, she knew a large clock was on top of a nearby building.

"Eight," Ellen said listlessly. Two hours had passed since Stephen had telephoned them to come right over; Gloria had gone ahead because Ellen's hair was not then dry enough to go out. And it still hadn't been when she had finally left, but she had dashed out anyway. And for what? To hurry up and wait.

She went back to her chair and sat down to gaze into space as Gloria, oddly enough, was now doing. Only Stephen was hugely pleased with life. He was apparently unaware of the funereal gloom; he sat on a straight chair, his legs propped apart, his back still in their direction, and fiddled with his typewriter as if it were a toy. He seemed as settled into his new life as if he had been built with the hotel. It was amazing what two thousand dollars could do. Of course Ellen hadn't actually seen the money, but he had had no reason to lie when he jubilantly telephoned his success. Gloria, like a fool, had blurted out her glad five-hundred-dollar tidings in answer, but Stephen had made no comment upon it, so perhaps hadn't heard it. Ellen, of course, had said nothing about her cousin's munificence or her evening there. The thought of her own duplicity brought a smile to her lips which went unnoticed in the heavy atmosphere. Was this the end of the triumvirate? Something told her it was; that explained, perhaps Gloria's unnatural cheerlessness. Or maybe she was upset because her john of the night before had not called; or jealous of Stephen's new alliance. She tingled with dread and impatience for somebody to say something, *do* something. As usual, they were attendant upon the whim of that selfish bastard. How could she love him?

But she knew she did. Her emotion sat lodged in her chest like a lump of gray clay, cold to the examining touch. Her love for him was a sick, clammy thing, but it was big; as huge as the world. Just thinking of its loathsomeness sent an incongruous flare of desire up to reach her mind, then it died. In its place came fear, stronger than ever, mingled with a tantalizing nameless quality striking her as vividly as a sexual flash, similar to it. It played over her like a ray, and she tore herself out of its path, using all of her diminished willpower, as if she had been looking over the edge of a precipice. Yes, it was like that. But something more too: and she recognized it as an ancient personal malaise, one she had first felt tug at her in childhood. When?

Then she remembered Rock Island; a place her family had taken her to one summer. Her memory of that place was acutely akin to what she had just felt. FEAR. Why? Why that place? She tried to think. It had been rock all right, but no island. Or hadn't it once been? Yes, of course. Geology and geography left over from years of school gave her child's memory an adult understanding: the river which had once surrounded a large piece of land or rock had been diverted for a dam—she even remembered the dam now—so that by the time she had seen Rock Island the name had no meaning. There had been only the rock riverbed, pock-marked with small shallow pools and occasional large ones; these were the ones she remembered. They had been dark and deep like the eyes of blue-eyed giants. She had been told people drowned in them all the time; it was very dangerous to swim. Why? she had wanted to know. Whirlpools, unseen, sucking the hapless swimmer down to the bowels of the earth, the body never to be recovered. Fear stood out all over her now like prickly goose pimples. Rock Island. Not Rock Hudson, whom he remotely resembled. But Rock Island McCoy.

"What are we going to do now?" she suddenly cried. Her voice shook with her anguish.

Gloria looked at her startled, and Stephen turned around to give her a curious stare. "Eat, I suppose," he said and turned back to jiggling the space bar on his typewriter.

"That isn't what I meant," Ellen said.

"I'm hungry. Aren't you hungry, Gloria?" he inquired without turning to ask.

"Yes," said Gloria.

"That settles it then." He stood up, giving his new pet a last tap, seeming reluctant to leave it, and said, "Where will it be? How about around here?" He stretched, yawned and smiled, mostly in Gloria's direction. "This is some pad, huh, ole Glory?"

Gloria nodded.

"I'm going to write me the best God damn American novel that ever got published."

Ellen cringed as if a pitcher of water had just been poured over her head; his arrogance was as chilling as an icy liquid. "You don't believe that, do you, Cornpone?" he asked Ellen, having caught her expression.

"Go ahead," she said.

"You chicks are both bugged because I've made out," he informed them.

"We're not," Gloria said stoutly.

"Yes, you are," he affirmed. "Look at Ethel Barrymore, Jr. Her face is as long as a whale's cock—"

"Longer," said Ellen acidly.

"—All because she's not the one getting the breaks."

Gloria and Ellen said nothing, so he blundered on into the decorous silence, rattling it like a bead curtain. "—Ellen will probably put her tail between her legs and creep home to Mother and holy Daddy-O now that she has been manumitted…" He paused to see if either of them knew what that meant, then went on. "'Please, Stephen,'" he mimicked her, "'please take me with you to New York. I'll do anything in the world to get on Broadway, or even off-Broadway'—"

"I never asked you to bring me to New York," Ellen said hotly. "You asked me to come."

"In a pig's eye. I couldn't shake you, baby." His eyes glittered with good humor, and he cast a look toward Gloria, his confederate. But Gloria's face was stern.

Ellen stood up, and when Stephen saw that she was about to cry he gave her a memorable splay-mouthed grin. It sickened her. "You're really an awful person," she muttered.

"How's that? Come again?" he said in a tight, cruel voice, and now his eyes glittered with anger, the mirth gone.

"I said you are an awful creature," she breathed.

He put his face up close to hers, his fist knotted. "Get this straight, doll. Nobody calls me a 'creature.'"

There was something downright comical in his cool rage. It was hammy. He bristled like a domesticated boar in a sty, covered with the mud in which he had been wallowing. She could nearly taste the acrid sourness of his whisky breath in her face. "Sorry," she said, curling her own small mouth at him, her eyes alert with defiance, "if I stepped on your clay feet."

And, as if mere words were a signal—any words she might have spoken—he crashed his clubbed fist into her jaw, and lunged in for the kill. He had her by the neck when he felt Gloria's hand on his shoulder. Her grip was as strong as a man's. He loosened his hold on Ellen's neck, almost playfully, as if he were merely teasing. Gloria could tell that the fight had gone out of him, but she pulled him off anyway, without a word.

The smile he gave to Gloria was that of a small boy to his mother, after a hard play. But her eyes were granite hard. "I'm cutting out," she said. "Are you coming, Ellen?"

There was no need to ask, for Ellen was shakily putting on her coat.

Stephen, jocular as ever, followed them to the door. "Is this the bitter end?" he asked.

Gloria eyed him coldly. "Sure it is, chum. We don't need you and you don't need us."

"You're damned right I don't. But drop around every now and then—anytime you get randy."

"Good ole satyriasis," Ellen murmured, her voice trembling.

"Is that what it was?" Stephen scratched his head innocently. "I thought you thought it was love."

Ellen sighed wearily, but the hand that felt her neck fluttered.

"Don't you want to fight? Come on, Tiger."

"Goodnight, Stephen," said Gloria.

"Sure you don't want to have dinner?" he asked, and was delighted to see that both looked as if this had taken away the last vestiges of their appetites.

They opened the door and walked out. He called after them as they went toward the elevator, "Give my regards to Chicago if you decide to head out that way."

They did not answer, and after grinning at their profiles which were turned aloofly away from him as they waited for the elevator, he apparently tired of his little joke, went back inside and slammed his door.

In the elevator, after inspecting Ellen's jaw to see if he'd really hurt her, Gloria murmured, "Don't take it too hard, kid. He don't mean it. He's not finished with you yet."

"I knew—I just knew when you told me about her this morning that Stephen was going to break it up."

"Aren't you glad, kid? There's other ways to get by. And maybe now he'll stop picking on you."

Ellen looked troubled, if not miserable, and her throat hurt.

"It'll be okay," Gloria said brightly in an effort to comfort her. "We've got my little nest egg—we can find some kind of joint for ourselves and get out of that lousy hotel. We can live it up. You won't have to worry about a thing."

Ellen looked at her in amazement. Gloria's generosity didn't surprise her, but the assumption that they would go on together— that she, Ellen, would on her own continue to be a shoplifter, perhaps joining Gloria in whoring—was dumb-founding.

"One thing I know," said Ellen quietly. "I'm not going back to Chicago or home or anywhere. I'm staying right here."

"We'll make quite a team," said Gloria, and this remark left no doubt in Ellen's mind as to what Gloria had in hers. Out on the street Gloria sought a drugstore. She wanted to call their hotel to see if there were any messages—specifically from Victor Rose, her john.

Ellen did not tell her how unlikely she thought this to be, but waited dumbly outside the booth, like a faithful pet. However, her agitation was unstilled. Stephen's violence with her, always a sign of sexual stimulation, was all the same dangerous, and this time had come about with surprising unpleasantness. She had no doubt that Stephen, amorously speaking, was not really through. The courage that had provoked his nasty taunting had come because he was secure in a way, since he had a stake now, but why was success accompanied by such obvious hatred of both of them? Or was it simply that he was released from fear? Perhaps Stephen was even more frightened than she and Gloria about the near miss in the store. Which figured. He was undoubtedly a real coward, for hadn't he let them take all the risks? And Ellen knew that Gloria had been really scared, though Gloria, when Stephen had phoned, had made it sound as if it were Ellen who was cracking up over it. At the time, listening to Gloria, Ellen had with swift perception seen the whole picture. To keep up their own courage they had put all the timorousness and fright on the doorstep of the novice. Why? Because being denizens of that twilight crime world themselves they knew the hard penalty of being inept. To Ellen it had been something of a lark—even this morning—each venture rather like a bit in drama class; unreal, fun. To her the danger had been negligible. What would have happened had they been caught? She knew very well. If that store detective had succeeded in hauling them upstairs to confront some executive or other, she *could* have produced her charge-a-plate—and wouldn't Gloria have been astonished?—and credentials. They would have given her a warning, maybe called her cousin, or even her parents, and she would have been let off. The worst that could happen to her would be that all concerned saw to it that she was banished from New York, sent home to reform. But Gloria, as sure as anything, would have been given a jail sentence, put right into the Black Maria and sent down to the Women's Detention House on Christopher and 10th.

Ellen sighed heavily. How cruel everything really was. The have-nots trying to exploit the haves. The haves truly succeeding in exploiting the have-nots. She felt ashamed and, for a moment, was tempted to walk out of the drugstore door, out of the twilight life, and disappear forever. But just then Gloria, exuberant, stepped out of the phone booth. "We've got a double-date, kid!" she cried, her eyes glowing. "Vic's bringing along a john for. you. We're to meet them at Sardi's yet! When they ditch their old ladies after the theater!"

## XIII

Gloria, who was as imperious as a dowager, assertive as a street urchin, had no trouble in getting a cab in spite of the theater crowd, and they jumped into it to go back to their hotel to dress up for their dates.

Gloria gushed and chattered as they rode along, sounding un-Gloria-like in the extreme, but the noises she was making were, however remarkable in being uncharacteristic, so familiar to Ellen who had heard many a Sweet Briar pal carry on so over a first date with the man that Ellen sat aside listening, as if Gloria were a dull book. Instead she thought intensely about herself and what was for her a new adventure which she was not at all sure she would not decline. First of all, she ached as if she had ulcers, all because of Stephen; it was bitter and hollow-making to have it all over, or at least put on this odious, crass basis. She wanted Romance again; she wanted it to be as it had been in Chicago. She wanted desperately again to think that Stephen had something "fine." She wanted to believe. Nobody would let her. Not even Gloria. Instead Gloria wanted to "fix her up." She had, perhaps, paid her a fine compliment in securing a john for her for tonight, but the question: do I really want to be a call girl, a whore? was no longer just academic.

Because she was an avid reader (though not always of the right books, as Stephen had pointed out) and because she was curious, mostly due to Gloria's proximity, she had read the spate of paperbacks on the life and times of the big city prostitute. They had made it sound not only pretty grim, but dull and confining, like being a nun or something. And once the racket got you, it had you, so the books had said. Very few had the guts to break away. They started out doing it for money or curiosity or both, and ended up doing it out of habit, like most things, which, of course, was weakness.

Ellen felt she had emerged from the world of petty crime practically unscathed; she had, if anything, sharpened her dramatic talents. But would she have emerged if Stephen had not decided to call it off? And had Stephen been a pimp instead of a small-time crook enamored of his own genius, wouldn't she have gone right along with him? "You're weak, Ellen Tate Terrill," her father, Frank Potts frequently orated at the dinner table which he regarded as a second pulpit, and she had always thoroughly agreed with him. But was it true, really? Her mother's family weren't like that.

"Cheer up, kid," Ellen heard Gloria say as Gloria gave her hand a warm squeeze. "This john—you don't have to go to bed with him if you don't like him."

"Suppose I do like him?"

Instead of answering, as Gloria thought the question was a joke not a serious inquiry, Gloria laughed and told her that was the spirit.

"What about money?" Ellen asked thoughtfully. "Suppose I don't want to take it."

Gloria thought this was another joke.

"I mean it," Ellen said. "I'm not sure this—well, doing this— is for me."

"Are you a virgin?" Gloria asked tersely, and Ellen knew that she had hurt Gloria's feelings.

"I see what you mean," Ellen murmured, and knew now she was morally committed to go, paradoxical as that might seem. She couldn't hurt Gloria, and, as Gloria had pointed out, she did not have to go to bed with the guy.

In full raiment, looking as non-whorish as most expensive whores, Gloria and Ellen arrived at Sardi's and upon the mention of Victor's name were deferentially escorted to his table.

Ellen was surprised to see that Victor looked almost as Gloria had described him. Indeed he was handsome, and looked enough like Robert Taylor at thirty-five to have been Robert Taylor. The man with him was plainly horrifying; even had he been alone and without such a brilliantly contrasting companion, Ellen would have shied away at his sight. He was all that Victor was not: old, obviously uncouth, however, rich (she could tell he was at least this by his horrid diamond ring, the expensive material of his flashy suit, and the white tie on white shirt which such men seemed to affect). He was, in addition, bald, pathetic and lecherous. The men stood up smiling, Ellen's date wearing a grin as sharp and glaring as an automobile's headlights. The girls sat down.

Now, thought Ellen, smiling and looking breathless, he's going to paw my knee, and he did. From then on, his every word and gesture she could have predicted, as if she looked over his shoulder at the script. He called her Blondie, he called her Gorgeous—which she was not and never would be—he ordered filet mignons without consulting her, as if this were a grand treat; he told her he was a leg man but that he appreciated breasts too and was glad she had both; he tried to tell the joke about the man from Mars who learns about making babies Earth-style until Victor stopped him; he said he seldom stayed up so late, but she was worth it; and he confessed with modest pride that he had made all his money in the manufacture of toilet seats.

The looks of s.o.s. which Ellen shot to Gloria at each of her companion's disclosures were lost like flares in the Atlantic. Victor and Gloria clearly were in love. Their fingers were laced together like trained woodbine. Their eyes sighted and focused like the shutter with the lens, and only murmurs, all private, came from their direction. Ellen was desperate. "Look," she said to Mr. whatever-his-name-was, "I have to go. I apologize for keeping you out so late, but I have an early rehearsal."

"Rehearsal? An actress," said her friend. "Maybe, girlie, I can do you some good in the theater."

"Doubtlessly," Ellen said frostily, and started drawing on her coat. Gloria and Victor still had not noticed.

"I mean it," he said seriously, trying to capture her hand with his beringed paw. "There's Logan Harper over there. You know who he is."

"Everybody knows who he is," Ellen said airily, not knowing, and not bothering to look either.

"He's a friend of mine. I could introduce you."

"I know him already, thank you," said Ellen, starting to rise. But it was too late. The toilet-seat maker had summoned his friend.

Perplexed, Ellen followed the gestures made between her squat companion and a white-haired, nice-looking man across the room. Finally, this social semaphore was supplemented by a note written by Ellen's friend to the man at whom he had gestured, and the written message was borne away by a waiter.

Logan Harper put in an immediate appearance. "Sam, it's good to see you," he said, clasping the hand of Ellen's john. And then he turned to Ellen. "Yes, you're right. I do think I know the young lady."

Ellen put a smile on her face and froze it there, not so much defying him to name her, but simply to play her part and get out.

"Now, wait," he said. "I *know* you're not Courtney Black-burn—"

"—I'm her cousin, remember?" and thus Ellen was saved by the bell.

"Of course, of course." Logan Harper pulled back a chair and sat down. "You look very, very much alike. Now I remember."

"Only we are really quite different—professionally, that is," Ellen said ingratiatingly, not realizing the double-entendre until after she had made it.

"Oh, yes. She's a very good comedy actress—"

"—And I have dramatic aspirations," Ellen supplied.

"Yes, yes, yes. What was that thing you were in—in stock—was it Virginia?" He snapped his fingers at his memory, trying to summon it like a dog.

Ellen said she thought he was mistaken; she had never been in stock in Virginia. Sam, pleased at first, watching their faces intently as though they were balls in a tennis match, now was bored. He excused himself to make a phone call.

As soon as he had gone, Ellen stood up again. "I'm sorry," she said to Mr. Harper, "I must go." Gloria looked at her dimly, but said nothing, and returned to her Victor, who immediately re-absorbed her like blotting paper applied to ink.

"You're going?" asked Logan Harper in regret and surprise.

Ellen nodded. "I must," she said confidingly, "before your friend comes back. All this is—well, I must."

"Let me put you in a cab."

"No, thank you. That's very kind, but I can manage."

However, he was on his feet, and as Ellen, having waved vaguely in Gloria's direction, started down the stairs, she knew the man was right behind her.

Outside, the street seemed dead and cool, just as were the theaters all around. It was somehow sweet. "It reminds me of a country town," Logan Harper said, as they waited for the doorman to bring a cab up to the marquee, and she suddenly remembered who Logan Harper was: someone far too important to insult.

As Logan Harper handed her into the cab, he said, "What address, my dear? I warn you I may use it for myself."

"In that case, the Plaza," Ellen returned laughingly, and added, "By the way, I don't live there, but I will tomorrow."

XIV

The driver wasn't sure whether she was drunk or just silly as she sat there giggling to herself, so he asked her if it was the Plaza or some other address.

This put a sober look on her face and then she said, "No, not the Plaza. Anyway I think I'll walk." Quickly she got out, put a bill into his hand, and was gone before he had a chance to think about it.

She walked east until the end of the block, then headed south, moving so swiftly that the men who turned to appraise her as a possible pickup decided she knew where she was headed and they would be wasting their time. Ellen's purposeful expression was the result of excitement; at the moment her pace would have been the same had she been en route to the gallows, which, in a sense, perhaps she was, because she was headed toward Stephen's hotel, drawn there as though mesmerized.

When she headed into the block on which the Sydney was located, she experienced a strong feeling of hesitation, something pulling back on her emotional reins, but she went right on. At the Sydney desk, she inquired for the house telephone, having no idea what she would say if Stephen were actually in his suite and picked up the phone. Nonetheless, she gave the operator his suite number.

"I just tried to phone you," he said, his voice rich and deep and quick; his wonderful voice.

"Oh?" said Ellen noncommittally.

Then he laughed. "What was wrong with you two tonight?

Didn't you know I was kidding?"

Ellen hesitated. "I guess we were both upset," she said cautiously. "It was a peculiar day."

"Yeah," he said, and she could hear him heave a sigh. "What are you doing?" he asked.

"Oh," she drawled, "nothing."

"Want to come up here?"

"Well—uh, maybe."

"I've been working," he said. "Writing. But I've had it for tonight—" he trailed off, cleared his throat, and added in a stiff almost sheepish voice, "I'd like to see you."

"I'd like to see you," she admitted wistfully.

"We haven't really seen each other for a long time—"

"No."

"Coming?"

"Um hm."

"How long will it take you to get down from your place?"

"Ten minutes probably," she lied.

"All right, sweet girl."

When Ellen hung up the house phone she found that the palms of her hands were wet. Nervously and rapidly, she left the Sydney lobby to go walk around the block a couple of times to pass the needed ten minutes.

Outside she realized, as if for the first time since she had been in New York with Stephen and Gloria, how reckless it was for a well-bred, well-dressed, well-protected pretty young girl to walk alone in this part of town at any hour. She felt an unaccustomed shyness and constraint which, mingled with her newfound reawakening of romantic anticipation for Stephen, made her glance around in awe at all she saw. It was exactly as if she had been asleep since they had left Chicago—even that momentary brush with the real and familiar at her cousin's had not stirred the mist.

The fog having cleared, and she knew it had been blown away by the succession of the day's events which culminated in her meeting with the critic Logan Harper, she felt strong and renewed, no longer the aimless love-logged blind girl who had followed Stephen's bidding into the labyrinth of an unknown kind of New York. First of all—tomorrow—she would move into the Plaza, by herself. She would get in touch with her family and tell them she was going to dramatic school here whether her father liked it or not. Then she would telephone Walter and Courtney and press them about meeting her cousin Sissy, or Courtney Blackbum, who might or might not help her. And she would certainly call Mr. Harper. However, she was going to do it right; she would ask him to the Plaza for cocktails, along with her cousins.

As for Gloria? Well. Gloria was Gloria, a girl who would always know her own mind. Gloria did what Gloria had to do, and what had been a temporary form of madness for Ellen was for Gloria a workable way of life, but one that could be discarded or amended at will. The look on the face of Victor Rose assured Gloria's immediate future. And Stephen—yes, that was going to be all right too. Being restored to—herself meant that she could love him in peace, without the frenzied dependence she had had before. She felt like a recuperating patient who learns for the first time just how sick he has really been. It was fantastic that yesterday, no, mere hours ago, she had considered entering a career as a prostitute and permanent shoplifter. What had made the difference, what had made her know that she was insane to think she was consigned to such a life? Money. It was as simple as that. First, Walter's check, then meeting Mr. Harper who had told her she looked like her successful cousin. He had made her remember her bank balance. She could live as she pleased. But she could not have remembered her money if her life had continued without an emotional point. Stephen had been it—and so unsatisfactorily—for so long, that he had almost made her forget there could be any other. Now she was glad for his rough, rude treatment, glad that he had tired of her clinging. If he had been gentle with her, if the idyll in Chicago had lasted, everything for her would have been finished. Now there was every chance that she really could become an actress, conceivably be good at it—

She turned the corner, caught a reflection of herself in the window of a cafeteria and walked on. I'm a good-looking girl, she thought to herself, but I don't want to be a girl. I want to be a woman. Her daddy was always saying she was a cute little girl— Stephen had always used to say, "Baby, you're a real girl girl." And tonight, hadn't Logan Harper called her a girl? What transformed a girl into a woman? She considered Logan Harper: he didn't appear to be the kind of man who would go in for "girls"—and certainly not "girlies," as did his fat friend Sam, her would-be john. Mr. Harper, undoubtedly married, equally undoubtedly had married a woman, not a girl; a wise, sweet, poised and pretty being who had gently ceased being a "lovely young creature" and had become a beautiful woman when the time came. And by now Hr. Harper was probably back and comfortably at home with her, and he was telling her about the opening of the new play which he had had to cover, and maybe mentioning that he had met Courtney Blackburn's cousin, among other people. When Logan Harper had handed her into the taxi, and they had had that badinage about the Plaza, somehow she had not been absolutely sure that his intentions were dishonorable, regardless of the circumstances under which they had met. She had gotten the impression that maybe he would be interested in helping her career— Well, he would, if she could manage it.

Ellen looked up and saw that she was at the entrance to the Sydney and she lightly went up the steps to go inside. A man brushed against her. She looked up; the brush had been deliberate.

He wasted no time; the suggestion he made was obscenely clear.

"No, thank you," she said as coldly as if he had just offered her a cigarette, and walked into the lobby.

Her hand was shaking badly as she lifted it to press the elevator button. She wanted to scream. I'll never, never walk alone in this part of town again, she swore to herself. Then she removed her finger from the elevator button and drifted away. What had made her promise herself that? If she kept that promise it meant never coming alone to this hotel again. Never seeing Stephen alone again, for where he lived the ground was taboo. She sat down in one of the lobby chairs to think. What would she have said to that man if she had been a woman, not just a girl? The same thing. What she had said was all right. Yes, Mrs. Logan Harper would have said that too. But would Mrs. Logan Harper have been found in the position where she would have to make such a reply? Possibly. New York was a big city, as interwoven with dangers for the protected as the unprotected—the difference being that the protected also cooperated with their protection by protecting themselves. Only on the rarest and most urgent occasion would a woman like Mrs. Harper—a lady if you will—venture alone into a hotel of this sort. She would not willingly court danger and indignity. Would such a woman take Stephen for a lover? Yes, certainly, if the various desperations of the mind, body and heart dictated; but, not on his terms. The terms would be hers.

Ellen walked out of the Sidney. I'm weak and bourgeois, she thought. Stephen had always said she was. Well, he was right if his definitions were. I'm weak enough to want to be a lady, she thought. And I can never be a lady with Stephen. I can only be a girl.

She told the taxi driver the address of her West Side hotel, knowing she was going back there for the last time, just as she was leaving the Sidney for the last time, and she wanted to cry. It was the same feeling she had had on her thirteenth birthday; she would never be twelve again.

Now, she thought sorrowfully, I can never tell Stephen all the things I wanted tonight so much to say. But she knew she couldn't tell him because they could no longer be shared—at least not with a Stephen. She couldn't afford to share; for the time being she would need all such nourishment for herself. Being weak, as he said she was, it would be madness to think that she could now have him on her own terms. Why, she hardly knew them yet herself! She had just landed, so to speak, and though she had her itinerary firmly in mind she still had not the faintest idea about directions.

But irresistibly his voice and image stood smiling and beckoning to her there in her mind. He was waiting for her now. Where had she found the impulse (she certainly could not call it courage) to just walk away? And why didn't she go back, knowing now what she had to do, for just one last time—just to feel him touch her, to lie in a bed with him again, his long, alive man's body stretched out beside her, making her feel so helpless, so loved, such a little girl. It was because she was through with being a little girl, that was why. That lovely little-girl helplessness, however appealing a state it was, had been the trap all along. Her daddy had built it for her— the first one—when she had truly been a little girl; built it as lovingly as if it had been a doll's house. And after she had squirmed out of that trap, which had grown too small, she had searched until she had found a man who could build her another: Stephen, her first love—her first non-incestuous love, at any rate.

She sighed and felt very tired; she wondered if Stephen would telephone her, in a rage if he did call, to find out what had happened to her. Probably not. It would not be in character. In such instances Stephen believed in letting them call him. Would she, and receive the cold shoulder she was sure he had reserved for her? No. She did not need to talk to him. If she couldn't see him there was certainly nothing to say. Now, still, he would be waiting, expecting her. When she didn't come would he be worried? No, but he would be amazed. How long would he go on, being sure she would arrive eventually? For never of course, would he think that she could deliberately fail to come. It was impossible to tell. Perhaps for hours. He was that sure of himself. He would have taken off his clothes, of course, preparatory for her coming, and would be lying on the bed, ready for her, ready to make love, for Stephen did like making love to her. She was certain of that. She felt sorry for him in that moment, as if he were a very small boy in for a big disappointment. But, oddly, she wasn't disappointed herself. Not then. Perhaps later—certainly earlier—and-so many, many times when he had casually let her down, had failed to show up for dates, or kept them only to send her away on some last-minute pretext. Or the times when he had been cold and had flatly said he found the mere thought of touching her repellent. She had silently put up with his moods and caprices, and when he was ardent, fond, she had gone along with that too, faithfully, grateful as a dog.

Tonight, she knew, he was ardent, fond. Why? He was certainly not sex-starved. He had probably had quite a night with his benefactress. Maybe tonight he craved young flesh.

Or maybe she and Gloria had frightened him by walking away.

Truth struck her a smart, flashing blow. Of course Stephen was frightened! Hadn't he said he had been joking with them? Stephen never for an instant meant to let either of his money-making girls go!

Now she wished the taxi driver would go faster, and carry her far far away in the other direction.

* * *

At approximately one o'clock in the morning, Stephen, who had finished the fifth of Scotch he had ordered earlier in anticipation of Ellen's visit, picked up the telephone and in a furry voice gave the hotel operator a number. It was not Ellen's.

After six rings a sleepy voice answered, and he said into the mouthpiece, as intimately as if he were speaking into an ear, "Come undress me."

The call was brief and successful, and some thirty minutes later Apple Ashby was at his bedside doing as he had requested. The whole while he was being unclothed, he sang in a sensual, nasal and off-key voice, "Oh, Western wind, where wilt thou blow? / The small rain down doth rain. / Christ, that my love were in my arms—"

This tickled Apple to death, and as he slid a heavy arm around her neck from time to time, and looked into her eyes, she giggled and said, "Just a minute, lover," and when he slapped her in the face, no love pat, and said, "What makes you think I'm singing to you?" she not only wriggled, but actually cooed with pleasure.

In spite of the fact that Stephen's potency was customarily diminished by alcohol, their mating was as vigorous, as noisy, as perfect as if it had been achieved on the back of a fence in the bold moonlight.

XV

Gloria sat listening to her man with an expression on her face so idiotic that Stephen could think of no better description for it than one favored by the ladies' magazines: she wore a look of bridelike radiance.

Victor Rose was not a bad joe; this Stephen had decided the night they first met, and so far at this second meeting he had been unable to find a reason for revising his opinion. He had purposely let Victor do most of the talking too, just to see if he had been right.

The conversation, of course, had been mostly about Florida, since that was where Gloria and Victor were bound—for two weeks of stolen but paid-for love, as Stephen had teasingly told Gloria when she called him and asked him to meet them at the airport. He had consented, for it was the only way Gloria would have a chance to see him before they left, though he found seeing people off a pastime to ridiculous that he couldn't believe that grown people actually went in for such things. "You won't be 'seeing us off,' honey," Gloria had assured him. "I'm doing this as a favor to you so we can talk about Ellen like you asked."

So far, however, Ellen's name had not been mentioned. But Stephen was in no hurry to bring it up. It could wait; all he wanted were the facts. At the moment all he knew was that Ellen didn't want to see him, that she had moved and didn't want him to know where, and that she was "all right"—a matter that did not concern him in the least. The first two conditions he had immediately interpreted upon hearing them to mean that somehow Ellen's family had caught up with her and that she was afraid to see him again—both because of what her folks would do and because of what she would do herself. And what she wouldn't do herself, he had thought upon hearing that he was now verboten, he would help her do once he got his mitts on her. For with Gloria having cut out, keeping Ellen was more important than ever. And if she were back in the family's graces, which naturally meant back in the chips, he could certainly use a girl like her. He knew having ole Glory face to face that ole Glory would give out and let him know how he could find Ellen again.

Gloria glanced at her watch, and Victor said, as if by plan, "Excuse me, darling. I'll go check about our return reservations," and politely left the two to talk.

They were sitting in the cocktail lounge and the ticket booth was quite a distance away which meant that even if Vicor didn't dawdle they would have a good ten minutes together at least. And ten minutes would be enough; more than enough.

"Victor give you that watch or did you lift it?" Stephen asked in idle malice.

"A little of both," Gloria said with a laugh. "If you call buying things wholesale stealing."

"May come in handy after the ball is over," Stephen observed. "Must have cost around a thou even wholesale. Let me see it."

Gloria took it off and handed it to him. "The ball's not going to be over," she told him. "Victor's going to get a divorce."

"Splendid," said Stephen. "Then he can marry me."

Gloria laughed good-naturedly. "All right," she said. "You'll see."

"Um hm," he said studying the watch. Then he handed it back. "Got any other gewgaws to show for this alliance?"

"Lots," she said. "Including an apartment when I get back."

"Well, *sir!*" Stephen nodded his head, surprised and impressed.

"In a respectable neighborhood, or more a chic-type neighborhood," she went on. "And with a roommate."

"That goes without saying. Hope you'll be very happy."

"I'm sure Ellen and I will."

For a moment he said nothing, then, "Has she already moved in?"

Gloria shook her head, hesitated a second and frustrated him by merely saying, "No."

Stephen gazed at her, his expression serious and contemplative. "I want her address, Glory."

"Okay," she said and handed him a piece of paper on which it was already written out. She had had it ready all the time.

He took it, gave it a glance, and put it in his jacket pocket.

"I'll call her up when I get back," he said.

"Wait until after midnight," Gloria advised.

"Midnight?"

"Yes. She's in a show."

"A show?"

"Yes. *Go to the Devil*, or something. Her cousin got her in. Victor and I saw it. She's real good, but they didn't give her much to say."

"I should think not," Stephen said. "Who's her cousin?"

Gloria told him all about it, or as much as she knew. She noticed his aghast expression turning to one of bitter envy as she elaborated on the facts: that Ellen had a steady boyfriend, also a Southerner and in the theater, someone her cousins knew; that she would continue living at the Plaza until the apartment was ready; that she almost never talked about Stephen.

"I'll look her up anyway," he said casually at the end of all this.

"You can try," Gloria said with a tiny touch of malice.

"It won't hurt nothing to try. How's Mrs. Silverman?"

Stephen made a weary gesture. "I have supplementary interests," he said. "Essie's just a feedbag—I do hope I don't shock you."

She waved aside his try at irony. "I didn't think it was a case of true love. How's the new one? Nice? Rich? Or both?"

"Village," he said. "La Vie Boheme. She has a bookshop and she's a tigress. We fight all the time. We may get married."

It was Gloria's turn to laugh. "Steve I know you. Are you making all this up?"

"No," he said, rather impatient that she hadn't believed him, and told her in detail how he had first met Apple Ashby; how he had gone back to see her the day after he had ditched her on the street, and how she had given him such a roll in the hay like he'd never had before. At the end he was rather disappointed that she made no enthusiastic or congratulatory comment.

Instead, she said, "Finish your writing yet?"

"Long since. It's about to set the world on fire."

"That's good," she said, and the conversation lagged. He could see that she was missing her Victor and uninterested in his career.

"You're really gone respectable, aren't you?" he asked with a hateful little smile.

"Oh, yes," she assured him. "I never did agree with you about stealing and things. I just did it. I didn't get any 'aesthetic kick' out of it like you used to say you did. Victor's what I always wanted."

"You and Ellen are two of a kind."

"I wish we were," she sighed and gave him a beautiful smile. "I'm trying."

"Well," he said, getting up, "as you know, I hate partings. I'm sure Victor will understand if you say good-bye to him for me. I couldn't bear—just couldn't bear, my dear—to see you two go flying off together in the wild blue yonder."

"You don't have to sound like a damned fairy about it," Gloria said. "Is your wrist getting limp?"

"You know how the Village is," he smirked, really letting his wrist go.

"You might make a good fag at that," she said deliberately spiteful.

His eyes grew hard, then extremely sad, almost pathetic. "I'll forget you said that, Glory."

"So will I," she said. "You'll always be my pal."

"You'll always be mine. I'll never forget what you did for me, Steve. You taught me how to be a lady."

"What's that?"

She made a gesture which he found rather charming. "Call me when I get back?"

"Sure. What's the number?"

She gave him the new address; he could get the number from Information.

"Here comes Victor. Have a good time. Make him treat you right."

"I will," she said, and watched as the two men met midway in the cocktail bar, shook hands, and parted. Victor, smiling, eager, his face full of what he felt for her, came toward her, and Stephen with a wave of his hand went off in the other direction.

* * *

Gloria, in her couturier-crafted bathing suit—made of-a fur blend material in a russet color which exactly matched her hair—was putting the finishing touches to her letter to Ellen. She pushed the sunglasses which she had forgotten to remove from her nose up to her forehead when she heard him laughing at her. "My crazy baby," said Victor, who had tiptoed in barefoot from the beach and had sneaked up behind her. He lifted her bodily from the French provincial chair in front of the desk to match and carried her into the damask paneled bedroom and put her tenderly on the silk spread of the Louis Quinze bed as if she were a boudoir doll.

"Don't you ever get tired of laughing at me?" she asked, smiling.

"Never," he declared. "You make me smile with my heart—just thinking about you," he murmured, his face close to hers. He was very tan now, Gloria noticed, and looking at him, she traced the firm bronzed laugh wrinkles around his eyes and then around his mouth, which continued to smile. He kissed her.

"I waited and waited," he said in her ear. "I couldn't wait any longer."

"Come on," said Gloria hopping up. "I'm ready now."

He pulled her back. "So am I," he whispered, and Gloria limply fell against him, closing her eyes, to shut out the intense ardor in his, as brilliant as the passion in her own.

Outside the brittle fronds of palm trees clattered in the hot breeze, making an unnoticed applause.

## XVI

Smiling at the spelling and Gloria's rather reckless penmanship and racy style, Ellen put the letter away. She looked up. "I'm sorry," she apologized to her cousins. "I didn't get a chance to read it before and I had to. I thought maybe it might be important."

"Was it?" asked Walter, busy at the bar with the inevitable "branch water" and Bourbon.

Ellen considered. "Yes, in a way." She supposed it was important to have Gloria's account of the meeting with Stephen— she had already had his, via the telephone; she had refused thus far to hear it in person.

"Is this the young lady you're going to be rooming with?"

"Yes," said Ellen.

"Hope we'll be meeting her soon," said Walter.

"Is she having a nice time in Florida?" Courtney wanted to know.

Ellen told her she sounded as if she was, and knew they were off on another probing session. She put a cool and equitable smile on her face for the interrogation. No, she didn't know why Gloria had chosen Miami Beach; yes, it was a funny sort of place for her to go. Yes, she was a gentile. No, she hadn't gone down on business—just a couple of weeks of sun. Did she have a private income? Yes, she did. Had Ellen said Gloria was from Chicago? No, some place in Oklahoma originally. "Oil," her cousins concluded.

But they hadn't concluded. Had Ellen said Gloria was older than she was? Yes, a few years. So she hadn't been going to the university with her then? No. "We just happened to meet," Ellen said casually, trying not to sound as fed up with all this as she really was. "You know how it is."

Courtney's prim expression indicated that Courtney did *not* know how it was. But she said no more. Instead she turned to disapproving of her husband; after all, she had a license to do that. "Bubber, you're going to make yourself sick drinking all that."

"Why, sugar," he said a little thickly. "You know I always hold my liquor."

"I won't tell you where you hold it," she said warningly, and Ellen thought: oh, God, here we go again!

But Walter seemed to have run out of repartee for the moment, so the three sat quietly, thoughtfully, in a sort of library silence.

Ellen knew they had asked her to dinner tonight, not because they found her such fun, but because they were her family and felt it their duty to keep up with her and see that she wasn't too lonely. The meeting with cousin Sissy had been a great failure, though cousin Sissy had helped her, also acting out of kinship duty, and had made it possible for Ellen to get the walk-on part which had just become open in her own play. At the theater, however, Ellen was like any other minor member of the cast and Sissy was like any other minor "star": they nodded. Too, Walter and Courtney had failed at creating a "romance" for Ellen with the young man from down home, also here in the theater.

"I have to go," Ellen said with a smile and got up.

"Why, hon, it's not even ten o'clock," Courtney said, standing up too, and quite willing for Ellen to take her leave. "I know, but I've got school tomorrow and then I have to dash straight fro m there to the theater—"

"They certainly don't give you much time to rest."

"Well, when you're leading a double life that's what you've got to expect," Ellen said with good cheer and no irony.

They smiled at her indulgently; she was indeed plucky, going to drama school, working and all.

As usual, Walter insisted on putting her in a cab, so she waited, already in her own hat and coat, while he got into his. She kissed Courtney's dry, powdery cheek and said goodnight.

In the elevator Walter and the operator exchanged views on the weather. Yes, Christmas would be here before you knew it.

Outside, Ellen paused to breathe in the sharp, dry air, and Walter remarked it was the kind of cold they had down home; without all that damned humidity which got into your bones. Ellen said yes, it certainly was.

When the cab came and Walter had handed Ellen in, she was extremely surprised to see him get in too and slam the door. "The Plaza," he told the driver. "I'm seeing my favorite cuz home."

The driver couldn't have cared less.

"Some of them like to talk, and some don't," Walter observed to Ellen, nodding at the driver's back. She laughed a little, feeling uncomfortable.

She had wanted immediately to say to him that it wasn't necessary for him to come along with her, but he had given her no chance. Now she didn't know how to say it; they were on their way.

"Don't you get lonesome and blue in that ole hotel room, Ellen Tate Terrill?" he asked lightly, as if he were winding up for a joke.

"No, I'm not in it enough," she said.

"Now, come on. You can tell your ole cuz."

"No, honest," she said again.

"How about your beaux?"

"Oh, those," she laughed uneasily. The truth of the matter was that she couldn't say she really had any. There was a funny-looking boy at school who took her to Schrafft's for hot fudge sundaes yet, and there was a dancer she had met through a boy in the cast who had rushed her for about two and a half minutes when he thought Courtney Blackburn's cousin might be able to do him some good.

"How about that fellow you said once followed you all the way from Chicago?"

Once in an off-guard moment she had fleetingly mentioned Stephen and had regretted it ever since. She had done so, however, to stop them from pressuring her about "beaux." Obviously, it had done little good. "I don't see him at all," she told her cousin.

"Have a spat?"

"Just drifted apart," she said, marveling at her own powers of understatement.

"He must have been a pretty poor sort of a fellow to let a girl like you do any drifting apart," Walter observed with what seemed to Ellen more than gallantry.

"I don't know what happened to him," she said and changed the subject by asking if he and Courtney were still planning to go down home for Christmas.

By the time Walter had thoroughly answered this they were at the Plaza. He handed her out, took himself out, and paid the bill.

"Now," he said, "for a little nightcap. Where do you suggest?"

"Look, Walter," she answered, "I really do have to——"

"No, no," he stopped her. "You've got to let your ole cuz buy you a drink. How about the Persian Room?"

"No," she said. She did not even want him that close to her sleeping quarters. "We can go up the street. There are lots of places on 58th."

Walter looked disappointed—obviously he had planned to give her and himself a little gala. Also, he regarded 58th Street rather mistrustfully. And of course he was right. Plenty of the drinking places they could go into were not quite "nice."

Ellen chose one which she knew was redeemed from this category by the fact that it had become a chic jazz hangout. They went in and the noise sprang at them like a pack of wild animals. Poor Walter looked miserable. "You particularly want to stay here?" he managed to make himself heard above the din.

She shook her head. No, that was being too cruel. They compromised by going to the bar in the Barbizon-Plaza.

Walter looked worn out from the effort, all of his ebullience gone. He also seemed to have sobered up considerably. He looked at her rather peevishly, she thought, his eyes cold and critical. Maybe he would be satisfied with just one drink and then let her go.

He gave their orders and said, "This is a nice place," having nothing else to say.

She knew he didn't really think so, but since it was not perfectly terrible he could compromise himself to this extent. "It's a nothing place," she said. "Just neutral."

"You don't come here much then."

"I don't go to any bars much," she said.

"That's good."

"I probably would, but I drink so badly."

"Why, I think you handle your liquor pretty well, young lady."

She smiled. The subject was tiresome, and why explain to him anyway that she was always on guard at his house and that she was perfectly capable of falling flat on her face if she had just an average number of martinis? He was staring at her hard, something new in his look; something she hadn't seen before. And it was neither family interest nor lust.

But whatever it was, Walter had changed his mind about talking about it.

To her own surprise, and certainly Walter's, she yawned.

"I'm so sorry," she apologized genuinely.

"We'd better be getting you back," he said.

"No, no," she said because she could see he was quietly hurt. "I'm not really sleepy. I just needed oxygen."

"Everybody does," Walter said. "As a matter of fact it's down-right good for you."

Ellen laughed gaily to make him feel good. "Speaking of oxygen, did I tell you that I'm going to Connecticut for Christmas?"

"I didn't know you had any friends up there, honey."

"Oh, yes, that's where my best friend at Sweet Briar's from. We haven't seen each other I don't know when."

"Well, that's nice. When you said you weren't going down home because of the play, Courtney and I felt real bad about it and were trying to think up some way we could see to it you had a real Christmas up here and not spend it by yourself."

"You all have been awfully sweet to me," Ellen said.

"No more than you deserve," he told her and closed his hand over hers on the table. Then, seeming to think better of himself, he relaxed his grip and gave her hand a pat. "We're real fond of our cuz," he said.

He's trying to control himself, Ellen thought, and felt relief. Her hand now, free, she picked up her drink, sipped it and gave him a smile to show tacit thanks and that she was fond of them too.

"Another?" Walter wanted to know. Her glass was now empty.

"I don't think so. I don't feel Bourbony tonight."

"I know just the thing," he said and caught the waiter's eye. "Here, waiter! Give this young lady a brandy alexander." He turned to Ellen. "Now that's a lovely drink for a non-Bourbon young lady. I wish I'd thought of it before." He told the waiter who was beaming at them with professional indulgence that he could fill his up again. On second thought, make it double. "Have to fortify myself for that lonely ride up to the Arctic," he added.

Walter loosened up and talked about the family quite amusingly and at length. Ellen found that she was enjoying herself. She asked questions from time to time, and from time to time. Walter broke off talking to reorder.

It was while she was finishing her fourth brandy alexander that she was aware that someone at a table just down from theirs was trying to get her attention. Then she recognized him. The odious toilet-seat maker, Sam. She cut her eyes away in a hurry, but he knew he had been momentarily successful in catching her eye, and was now waving to her. In a minute Walter would notice.

"Don't you feel well?" Walter said suddenly.

So I look it too, she thought. She put her head in her hands. "Your face is all white. I'll get the bill."

But when Walter stood up Sam also stood up and came over. Walter gave him a puzzled cool look.

"Hello, girlie," said Sam. "I tried to call you after you ran out on me that night, but your friend Gloria answered and said you'd moved. I even asked Logan Harper if he'd seen you."

Walter, at least, responded to the look of horror on Ellen's face. "Is this gentleman a friend of yours, Ellen?"

She introduced them in. an almost inaudible voice, her words racing. "Excuse me," she added. "We were just leaving."

"How about your telephone number before you go?" Sam asked unabashed.

Rather blindly Ellen shook her head and put her arms into the coat Walter was holding for her.

"Good evening, sir," Walter told him with frosty hauteur, and putting his hand under Ellen's elbow, he steered her out. Silently, they walked in the cold harsh night. The lights of Sixth Avenue and 58th Street were almost more than Ellen could bear. She longed for the dark. She closed her eyes, trying to will herself into the country. A field with snow on the ground.

"You want to talk about it?" Walter asked quietly.

She shook her head miserably. "It's just me," she tried to explain. "That person is—nothing."

"I didn't get his name," Walter said. Ellen repeated it for him.

"And wasn't that Logan Harper he mentioned the one Suster and I met?"

"Yes," Ellen said faintly. "I met him the night I met Mr. Harper in Sardi's."

"Well that's not so bad then," Walter said. "But that fellow was kind of flashy looking. Is he connected with the theater too?"

Ellen said that he wasn't. "Is he a friend of Gloria's?"

"No.·He just knows Mr. Harper."

"He said he tried to call you somewhere. Were you and Gloria staying some place together?"

"Yes," Ellen admitted. "We had a hotel room together."

Walter took this news without comment, but apparently decided not to brood about it. "You little rascal," he said at last. "You'd been in New York some time, hadn't you?"

She nodded.

"I just knew it. I told Courtney I suspected something was going on that first night we saw you. And I was right about your being in trouble, wasn't I?"

"Yes, you were right, and I never did get a chance to thank you properly for that check."

"But you didn't cash it."

"No."

"So it wasn't money trouble."

Ellen couldn't make herself reply. They walked along silently, and Walter kept trying to look in her face.

Then he spoke again. "Courtney and I thought your Mr. Harper was someone you knew because of your acting. Sissy told us he stood very high in his profession. He seemed like an agreeable fellow—we didn't think there was anything wrong about him—but hon, he must be a whole heap older than you—"

"Walter," Ellen cried, tears in her eyes. "I barely know Logan Harper. I haven't seen him more than three times in my life. When I met him, once with you, and when he introduced me at the school."

"I'm sorry," said Walter and she knew he was deeply wounded.

When they reached the Plaza, he took her to the door, and aside from having touched her elbow to help her up the steps, he did not touch her again. Instead he tipped his hat. "Good night, Ellen. We enjoyed having you for dinner and I thank you for joining me for a drink."

Her lashes still wet, but the tears gone, she looked into his sober, well-bred face and thanked him.

But she didn't think she was going to make it upstairs in time before the real cloudburst came.

XVII

One of her best customers, now holding volume I of the Variorum Shakespeare in his gloved hand in that possessive way that usually indicated a sale about to be made, had just remarked to Apple Applebaum (as Stephen now called her, since at least the latter was her real name) that if it wasn't going to be a white Christmas it was certain to be a cold one. She had laughed like anything, her eager avarice bubbling through the usual gagging whinnying sound which Stephen thought so appalling to have to identify as laughter. He glowered now, at her, at everybody in the store, and thought to himself if he had to hear anymore bookshop wits or listen to any more of Miss Applebaum's distressing eruptions of mirth, he would knock out every tooth in the place, true, eye, wisdom, and false.

The little book store was crowded, for it was Christmas eve, and all the people who had put off their shopping until the last minute, or who, in desperation, had decided they couldn't think of anything at all for so-and-so except maybe a book, had crowded in. The place was full of uptown faces, faces not to be seen again ever, in all probability, and certainly not until a year from now. Of course there were the regulars too, such as the old party in the coat with the ratty fur collar holding the Shakespeare in his hand, and Apple Ashby was in Seventh Heaven, looking like the Chock full o'Nuts lady on TV smiling into her golden shower. Stephen hated it all. He didn't know why he sat there. Or rather he did know why he sat there. He couldn't go back to the Sydney for the simple reason that he had been locked out—he, Stephen McCoy, locked out

129

of a hotel room—for nonpayment of rent. Locked inside with the few possessions which were not locked in the vaults of the Provident Loan Society was his four-hundred-page manuscript, beautifully typed, now a little dogeared from handling by people who were going to reject in anyway— "A fantastic tale, Mr. McCoy, but the credibility is doubtful—" What an incomparably lovely use of the English language that was! "—Entirely convincing about the thefts and other minor lawlessness, but the girls don't come through as real people...." Small wonder! "—The protagonists all seem completely amoral, without a goal. No one of them seems to realize that there are other ways to live—" The protagonists! Jesus Christ! What kind of morons were these editors? Didn't anybody ever teach them English? Poor Fowler! He'd tried so hard! But the one guy who had written "—Mr. McCoy, we feel that if you would write from your own experience—" had really done the trick. They were clearly all fools. After that one, things had really started to go. First of all the old Silverman sow. Not content with once a week, and cutting it down to a hundred bucks (he never had gotten the balance of the promised two thousand), she had to get jealous as well as stingy. But not too stingy to hire the private detective who gave her a full report about a certain Miss Apple Ashby who ran a very bohemian-type Village bookshop frequented by "marijuana addicts, intellectuals, and other suspicious characters," and with whom Mr. S. McCoy was known to be openly consorting. The report stated that he spent approximately one night a week in his hotel, and five he spent in Miss Ashby's apartment on Jones Street. The seventh night Mrs. Silverman could account for herself.

"Stevvie, I don't want that this should hurt you," Essie had said, her hand and voice trembling as she put the report into his hand. If her eyes could have done it, they would have trembled too.

He had read it coldly and handed it back. "Well?" he had said.

"No more money, Stevie. You didn't do right. Now we'll see if you like me like you say. Now we'll see if you come visit me just for me."

"No, we won't see," Stephen had said. "You've had it."

He thought she was going to cry. Her lip trembled. "But Stevie, after all."

"After all what?" he wanted to know, his lip curled.

"We have so much in common," she pleaded.

"I'm not common," he had said and stomped out.

But he knew he was common all the same. Maybe not so common as Esther Silverman, but—well, not in Ellen's class. Hearing the Appletree's laughter again at some other unfresh customer sally, he remembered Silver Ellen, silver voice, silver hair, silver bank account. A sterling girl. He had tried to get her on the phone last week. Out, Gloria had said. Yes, Ellen seemed to have landed on her feet. Had hit Cholly Knickerbocker's column, no less. Yes, yes, Ellen was probably on the verge of becoming a big name in the theater. Then Stephen had given Gloria the coarse laugh that she had once known and liked so well accompanied by an expletive that so completely became it that he always thought of the two together, like a heroic couplet. "Don't you say 'horse shit' to me!" Gloria had shouted into the phone, and even as he was rejoining with a pleasant, "Okay, your ladyshit," she was hanging up on him.

And now Stephen sat like an old man—old man Gerontion—in a corner of a bookshop as noisy and fulsome as Gerontion's windy house, dejected, if you will, rejected, if you will, bored and annoyed even with his memories.

Apple was determined to squeeze the last penny from her Christmas rush, light as a snow flurry compared to other businesses, but she loved money as much as any Hetty Green female who had ever soiled her hands with the Great American Dollar. And this week she was keeping the shop open until midnight. The hour was now eleven, and though the browsers and buyers milled around showing signs of fatigue, Apple was as fresh as a whirling dervish at the start of an Arab funeral. Stephen knew the stock perfectly—no difficult feat, as the shop was small—and in the first days of their "love" had taken an interest in lending a hand with the customers; had, in a sense, taken over, or so she had hotly accused him. But he had completely lost interest in playing bookseller by Christmastime, and took a contrary pleasure in sitting around, getting in the way and doing nothing.

Their affair had almost run its course; he, himself, had been bored by her almost from the beginning, bored, that is, when he wasn't irritated, and now the dissatisfaction had spread to her. They were like an old, old married couple, having jammed a lifetime of connubial experience into a matter of weeks. He knew her history thoroughly—or could have if he'd bothered to listen—and she thought she knew his. It was true that she knew things none of the others had known, for she was by nature as curious as a cat; because she was also in many ways as cozy as a cat their curious depth of domesticity had come about. But now both were spiritually ready for a divorce. But there are other things in this life besides spirit and among these other things is money.

Stephen had dutifully paid his own way with her at first, and had the done "nice" things which girls like. But he had sensed the presence of the Widow Silverman's detective even before he had been actually hired, and little by little Stephen had reduced the quantity and quality of his favors to Apple. Their dinners together became "Dutch treats," though the appellation was questionable. This had perhaps aroused Apple's suspicions, but it was not until his "income" ceased altogether and he had begun to apply to her for small loans that she had become unfriendly about it. To save his future skin, having no pride where money was concerned, he had popped this and that and the other into the pawnshop so she would not see that he was as broke as he really was. He would have liked then to go back to the "old life" to some degree, but he couldn't make it alone; the one time he tried he had come so close to being caught that he had put the coveted object back on the counter and had gone out, badly shaken. Trying to reassemble the troupe was laughably impossible. Both Ellen and Gloria were in other orbits, and very successful, he supposed, in their own way. Ellen had her part in this play and Gloria was living with her john, or at least he was keeping her. Gloria still proudly asserted that his intentions were honorable, or would be as soon as he could get a divorce. And more of that sort of jazz, mainly to believe it herself. So neither was of much good to him, though Gloria was good for a liberal touch now and again.

Tonight at dinner Stephen had indicated to Apple that he was now ready to move into her apartment, as she had repeatedly asked him to do. "Why?" she had wanted to know, and with his candid charm, he had told her. To his dismay she had shaken her head. "I'm not keeping any starving artists," she had said. "You can write the great American novel at somebody else's expense."

Stephen assured her he was through with all that; now, he went on, he was ready to get a job. Of course she had wanted to know what kind, and though he had more or less convinced himself in outlining his plans, obviously he had not convinced her. Since dinner she had not spoken to him.

Had it been less cold outside, and had he had enough money to go off and get soused somewhere, he would have long since gotten the hell out of there, Christmas eve or no. Apple had planned to open their presents tonight, seated like infants in their Dr. Denton's under the tree. Which was a crock. She didn't know it, but he planned to cut out as soon as he was able to get Gloria on the phone and go up there and get some jack. And maybe a roll in the hay for auld lang syne if he could talk her out of that fidelity bit. But he couldn't call until midnight; Gloria's Victor would still be there. So far, it had been a lousy Christmas eve.

He remembered others; some better, some worse. Those spent with his grandmother in Ohio were the worst. Ten of them altogether. Once she had given him an orange in his stocking. When he was twelve his new stepfather, with whom he was then living, had literally given him ashes. And one Christmas—had he been sixteen?—he had spent in jail. And several in the Army; those were not so bad. He had felt perhaps less sorry for himself than the other slobs. Where were the good Christmas eves? One, he remembered, with a girl—a tender star of a girl, rather like Ellen, except her teeth were bad and hence her breath and she was a whore. What mattered if you had pushed yourself and worked yourself and polished your mind to be diamond sharp and knew more than ninety percent of the creeps you saw in the subway or riding in Cadillacs if you'd had nothing but lousy Christmas eves? He felt ready to cry.

He stood up, taut with anguish and self-pity and walked out of the door. "Where are you going?" Apple cried in alarm, just as she had that first time.

"Uptown," he answered just as he had answered the first time too.

As he stood in front of the apartment house, shivering in his fall coat not made for rugged weather, he once again debated calling up before he went in. Gloria expected him to, for it could be very awkward for everybody. Not only might he run into Victor, but there was Ellen. Though she would speak to him on the phone, she would no longer see him. He quite understood and it didn't make much difference to him. For a moment he watched the traffic at the other end of the street—on Park Avenue—even the cars seemed to know Christmas was here. What, he wondered, was that bastard in the black Continental going to give his car for Christmas? A nice tankful of gas would be most suitable for it and Stephen too. Going inside, nodding to the wary, impeccably uniformed lackeys who stood about the lobby, he experienced an inner glow of excitement at the thought of all that good free hooch Gloria kept upstairs.

He stepped into the elevator and with the ease and authority he had acquired in the old days he gave Gloria's name and floor and was borne upward without any questions asked.

As he rang the bell he felt suddenly lightheaded. The heat from the building had met the cold from the street and produced their inevitable chemical effect. He grinned to himself, feeling drunk already, and was not even slightly surprised when Ellen opened the door.

At first she didn't say anything, but stood there looking slim and poised and beautiful as a Christmas carol sounded. Then came her voice, so perfect for the season. "Hello, Stephen. I'm afraid Gloria is out."

"But you're not," he said, his eyes friendly to the point of merriment, lively with appreciation of her appearance.

"I almost am," she said with a little awkward laugh. "I was just going to bed. I have to get up early."

"Rehearsals on Christmas day?"

She shook her head and laughed her nervous but beautiful laugh again. "Connecticut," she said simply.

Stephen looked at her. He longed to ask her to laugh just once more, to say something to make her do it. He couldn't think of the right thing. "When will Gloria be in?"

Ellen told him that she couldn't say and he knew she was waiting for him to leave.

"I didn't come to see Gloria necessarily," he said, having had a sudden inspiration. "I'm a carol singer. I came to sing a carol to the household.”

She laughed a little again. “Thank you. Maybe next Christmas.”

“What? No wassail bowl for the weary carol singer?”

“What’s a wassail bowl?”

“Ignorant Southerner.”

“Goodnight, Stephen.”

“Goodnight.”

But he didn’t move and she didn’t shut the door. “All right,” she said. “A Christmas drink.”

XVIII

He walked into the apartment as if he owned the place, and made straight for the bar, poured himself a tumbler of Scotch, downed it at once. Then he looked up mischievously into the cold staring disapproval on Ellen's face and belched. He patted his offending mouth politely, and then, giving his stomach a hearty pound said, "There. That's better."

Without waiting for an invitation, as he was doubtful if one would come, he threw off his overcoat and tossed it over a couch and sat down. "I never can get over it," he commented looking around, "to think you and Glory decorated this salon all by yourselves."

"I didn't have much to do with it," Ellen said quietly. "Victor has awfully good taste. You know perfectly well it's their apartment really. I'll move when they get married."

"They'll tear down the building for old age before that happens," he cried gleefully.

But Ellen didn't think the joke huge or funny. She examined her folded hands. There was no need to ask Stephen why he was being so nasty; no need and no use. Further, he knew perfectly well that she simply would not discuss Gloria's life with him. She had told him that often enough over the telephone. Among other things. But still—and she stole a short look at him—she was glad to see him after all this time. It gave her a peculiar pleasure; a warmth and a sadness. It was like going back to Sweet Briar or somewhere and seeing your old room again where you had been happy and miserable; now it couldn't hurt you or touch you anymore.

Stephen, restless as ever, was up pacing the floor, looking at this and that, handling things, with his impudent proprietary way. He was like a handsome street urchin grown up. Not so far from the truth at that. Then she felt an old finger of pity touch her.

"Are you staying in the city for Christmas?" she asked.

"Yes, I'm 'staying in the city for Christmas,'" he mimicked her prissily.

It failed to make her mad. Instead she smiled. Stephen had always been a good mime. "Well, have a happy, as Carol Reed says."

"Aaah, television!" he said in disgust. "You're just like all the rest of them. A real square cat. I used to think you had some sense—sense and sensitivity. I'll bet you even think television is our greatest cultural invention to date."

"I'll bet I think it's old hat to knock it," Ellen said placidly. "Anyway, I've seen you enthuse over a red-hot TV program many a time."

"'Enthuse,' my dear erudite young friend, is not one of the words which disgraces the English language."

"It's in the dictionary," she said defiantly, and suddenly realized that this scrapping was almost a literal playback of their pre-bed conversations in Chicago. The days of stained innocence, of good unhealthy fun.

"Where's your damned dictionary!" he demanded, but she gave him a listless shrug.

"Don't be so aggressive," she told him.

"All right. I'll find it myself—if there *is* one!"

He left the living room and she ran after him, slightly excited by the deceptive hostility and sarcasm, but annoyed that he would invade her bedroom, paw over her personal things, in order to satisfy one of his arrogant whims.

As he went to her bookcase and bent over to rapidly inspect its contents, she simply hit him. It was not a hard blow, but it was sharp, and he put his hand on his sleeve in surprise, as if to absorb the warmth of the smarting pain into his hand. His eyes glittered at her like black, wet mud. He gave her a shove which sent her back against a boudoir chair, hurting her leg.

Panting, she watched him, torn between helplessness and action. As she well knew from experience, Stephen played hard. He glanced at her briefly, aware of her heavy breathing, and continued to peruse her book collection.

The moment, she knew, had passed. Now she was safe. She had bypassed the danger point. If she had gone at him, clawing and kicking as she had been tempted to do, they would have fought like mating cats; and she would have ended up on the bed, with Stephen on top of her. Inevitable.

Without a word, she turned and left the bedroom.

He returned soberly a few minutes later with her Webster's Collegiate Dictionary in his large hand. He sat down and consulted it privately, without interest. He did not bother to share his findings. It had all been a game anyway.

"I'm very tired, Stephen," she said.

He made no reply, simply picked up his coat and draped it over his shoulder as he walked to the door.

Looking at his back, she experienced a feeling of endless sadness. She had loved him so much! She got up and walked after him to the door. At least she could make a pretense of being unshaken by all this.

"I'm sorry I'm so tired," she offered in a small voice.

"I'll bet you are," he said scornfully.

He opened the door. Clearly he had said all he intended; this did not include goodnight.

"Goodnight," she said anyway.

He turned and gave her a summary look, so scathing, so awful in its bitterness that she took a step backward.

Then as if he were suddenly dying, his body fell toward her, clutching at her, frantic, his fingers like steel, and she realized he was sobbing. "My Ellen, my Ellen, my Ellen," he seemed to be saying as he stood there in the doorway, his great shoulders heaving, hanging on to her for support. His wet face hungrily found hers, his mouth blindly sought her mouth, and he kissed her as she had always wanted him to kiss her, a paroxysm of passion thundering through his body, so that her body shuddered too from the impact.

But the switch from his craving maternal need for her to a craving love desire had been too quick, and she felt no answering urge. She stood rather awkwardly holding his body as if he were suffering from a convulsion, wondering what to do next.

He had ceased to blubber, but he was still incoherent with emotion, his words thick and fast between the kisses he grabbed from her, thick and fast also. "This is the way I've always felt—love you…oh, Ellen, Ellen—why did you do it?—this is right"—were among the phrases she could make out.

His confession excited her, but her response was a feeling of gladness, well-being, more akin to the surge of patriotism a school child feels at a parade, her heart triumphant with lilting pride, marching along.

Stephen seemed to sense at last that she wasn't with him, and once sure of it, he simply left off, dropped his arms and stood up straight. Coolly, he surveyed her, produced a handkerchief and blew his nose into it as if it were a trumpet. "Sorry," he said, "for the waterworks. All a great bore. Touching little scene, wasn't it?"

"It wasn't a great bore," she murmured.

"No?" he said stingingly. "Whatever made me think you thought so?"

She shook her head, as if he had shamed her.

"You God damned icy bitch," he said with slow loathing.

"No, Stephen," she faltered. She tried to touch his arm.

He jerked it away.

He clenched his fist, his eyes blazing. "I think I'll kill you!"

She cowered away from him, then recovered herself. "Either you come in and have one last drink and behave yourself, or go away."

Rudely, he pushed past her. The mention of liquor, she knew, had aroused another craving. Of course he would need a drink. He was at the bar, pouring it already, as unaware and as uncaring of her now as a savage is of the missionary he has trussed up for the stewing pot.

After his second shot, which seemed to take the edge off his insatiety, he sat down, glass in hand and began to peruse her dictionary again. From time to time, he permitted himself a private little smile, amused here and there by what he read. Stephen fancied himself, or had at the University of Chicago, as a philologist; as if the English language had been especially created for his own use and study.

Ellen watched him silently, thinking that he was really quite mad, and wondering what he would do next. She had no intention of sitting there all night while he read to himself and got soused on their liquor. On the other hand, she couldn't very well go to bed. Gloria and Vic had gone to a party and might not come back at all. Frequently, they spent a night together in a hotel. Victor considered it bad manners to fornicate when Ellen was in the house, even if it was really his house, which both amused and touched Ellen in the circumstances. He had apparently had both the need and the success of whitewashing Gloria completely. But he was a determined man and in love. Gloria had responded beautifully. Even she didn't seem to remember that she had ever been a whore.

Still taking no notice of her whatsoever, Stephen got up and now then to replenish his drink which he would take back to his chair and his reading matter. Ellen yawned openly once and hiccoughed in the process. He gave her a sharp unseeing glance, like a student frowning at some unknown noisemaker in the library, and went right back to his reading. She fidgeted, crossed and re-crossed her legs, trying to find a comfortable position. Her knee still hurt from the push Stephen had given her in the bedroom. She stood up and strolled to the bar, measuring with her eye the amount of Scotch he had consumed. Enough to make a skunk drunk. Then she sat back down and did nothing.

In her mind, she began to phrase sentences with which to dismiss him, to say she was going to bed. Cowardice or reluctance did not prevent her from voicing any of the dozen or so that came to her, but something did. She didn't know what. It was a mixture of curiosity and laziness; she wanted to see on the one hand just how long he and his audacity would hold out; on the other it was simply too much trouble to tell him to go.

"Fix you a little drinkypoo?" he surprised her by saying. She had been so engrossed in her dull musings that she had neither seen nor heard him get up and come over to her where he stood now, looking down at her, the picture of good humor and jocularity, his expression intimate and fond. "Yes, I wouldn't mind something to drink," she responded unthinking, and as he went to fix her Bourbon—he knew what she liked—she was rather sorry.

He came back and sat down beside her on the couch and gave her her drink. "Want to go to bed with me?" he asked as if he were making a private joke.

She laughed. "What do you think?"

"I think you do," he replied in this new teasing way. "But I don't think you will."

"I don't either," Ellen said, her tone as light and easy as his own.

They grinned at each other over their drinks. "Good old Ellen," he squeezed her hand. "It was fun, wasn't it—when it was fun?"

"Yes," she agreed. "The best."

"The very best." He tightened his pressure on her hand. "I'd better drink up and get going so you can get some sleep," he said considerately. "Where did you say you're spending Christmas?"

She told him and asked about his again.

"Oh, I'll spend it with Apple," he told her and looked at her rather slyly to see if the name meant anything to her.

"That's the girl you told Gloria you were going to marry." He gave a huge roistering laugh of delight, as if it were some kind of private celebration. "Me marry *that* one? Why, honey-child I'd sooner marry the Widow Silverman—or you." Ellen ignored this dig and inquired about Essie. Stephen explained her away in a minute. "No, I've decided to be faithful to you," he told her banteringly.

About time, she thought rather wistfully, but didn't mean it to herself. "How about Apple?" she parried.

"You ever try shacking up with a peafowl? She's got a voice like a—it, well, it beggars description, even from an ole litterateur, raconteur like me. My book has been soundly rejected, you know," he added, looking at her sadly. "They say it's neither Great nor Novel, just possibly American."

"That's awful, Stephen."

"You bet your boots it is, baby. And on top of that I'm flat broke."

Ellen waited for him to go on, feeling cautious about saying anything just then herself. Her desire was to offer him money then and there, but she was determined not to go crazy again, even to that extent.

Stephen's face was heavy with brooding. Ellen looked at him with love in her eyes which he turned suddenly and saw. "Don't worry, baby doll," he said huskily, squeezing her hand again. "I'm into you for more than I care to count. I won't bother you anymore."

"Stephen," she murmured brokenly.

He put his arm around her, and kissed her lips, as if he were kissing a child. Then he released her, but continued to gaze into her face. "Yes, you were the best," he said.

Then he stood up. "One for the road? May I?" he asked charmingly, indicating his glass. "Then I'll let the thespian go to bed."

"Would you like to see the play?" she asked impulsively. "I'm hardly in it, but maybe you'd like to see it. It's not bad."

"Sure, I'll see it. Maybe meet your famous cousin," he gave her a broad wink. "Think you can fix me up?"

"Courtney Blackburn and I aren't particular friends," she said evasively, feeling uneasy.

"No?" he said in surprise. "Then how come she's furthering your career?"

Ellen told him how it all came about; even told him about Logan Harper's having used his influence to get her in this acting class that everybody was dead to be in.

"So he's your new lover boy," Stephen concluded. "Gloria mentioned him."

"Oh, no," Ellen exclaimed with a frown and again explained the whole thing to Stephen, emphasizing this time the part her other cousins had played in her good fortune.

"Are they the ones you won't introduce Gloria to?"

Ellen looked uncomfortable. "I've never refused to introduce her. It just never has happened, that's all."

"But she wouldn't like them, or they her?" he suggested evilly.

She made an offhand gesture, trying to cover her embarrassment, when he changed his tone completely.

"That's okay, kid. You don't have to explain. I understand," he said quietly. "I don't blame you, and I don't think Gloria really does either. People aren't responsible for their families. My stepfather was a snob too. Did I ever tell you about him? He tried to make me over into a little gentleman. He might have even succeeded if my old lady hadn't decided to divorce him for a creep who ran a bowling alley. Then I was converted from Little Lord Fauntleroy to Little Lord Pinboy. Quite a change." He gave her a disarming, slightly sad smile. "You and Gloria are really first-rate people," she said.

"The best."

Stephen smiled at her fondly. "Maybe Gloria, but I'm not. I've got a mean streak in me. I don't know what happens. I don't mean to be cruel. I don't even enjoy it when I first do something hurting or blurt something out I had no intention of saying. Then it gets a grip on me, and I go wild. It's a form of intoxication—I get carried away. Then when it's all over I'm sorry about it. Like now."

She looked at him questioningly to see if he meant her, and by way of answer he put his hand around her face and lifted it up. Then he kissed her. "If I ever loved a living soul, I love you, Ellen," he whispered."

"I love you, Stephen," she whispered back, and they sat there, arms about each other, kissing each other's mouths and eyes.

# XIX

In tacit understanding, they rose, arms still about each other, and went back in tandem to Ellen's bedroom, filled with mutual love and desire.

Ellen let Stephen undress her, which he did slowly, lovingly, pausing to kiss her on each part of her anatomy he unclothed. She was bursting herself with love of him, surfeited and transported by it as if it were a powerful drug. Her pulses throbbed and her heart beat as if her whole body were a giant, quivering machine, a huge plane, ready to take off.

And at last when Stephen was actually there making love to her, she found with disappointment that the anticipation would not abate, would not let her abandon herself to the unthinking animal state requisite for satisfying her body. Her mind kept crying out for more, for she could not believe that it was actually happening to her again at last. And in a few minutes it would be all over, and she had hardly begun. She clung to him fiercely, and he seemed to understand her desire, though he had never let such a thing interfere with his own satisfaction before. But it was no good, and finally he whispered, exhausted, panting, "It's no good, baby. I can't wait."

Ellen felt him leave her and she heard herself cry out, brokenly, grief-stricken. He felt for her hand and squeezed it hard. "There's always next time," he whispered.

But she continued quietly sobbing, released at least by her tears. He put his arms around her gently, to comfort her and after a while, the crying stopped.

"I've got to cut out, baby," he murmured in her ear. "You've got to get some sleep."

"No, Stephen, no!" She hung on to him.

He chuckled a little. "Honey, I'll be back. I'll come back to-morrow night."

She sighed and rolled over on her back away from him. "I'll try to get away. I'll tell them I have to catch an early train because of rehearsals."

"All right," he said genially.

He was now getting into his clothes, moving around in the semi-dark, putting them on as he found them.

"I don't mind if you turn on the light," she told him.

"I mind," he said. "I don't want you to see my pot belly."

"Oh, Stephen, you crazy thing!" she cried happily and threw a pillow at him to let him know she didn't care how he looked so long as he was there. "Anyway," she added, propping herself on an elbow. "You don't have a pot. You won't have for years and years. I'll let you know when you're getting a pot."

"Maybe you won't be around then," he suggested.

"I'll be around, don't you worry," she said. "Even if I'm dead."

"Necrophilia is not one of my vices. Besides, you'll run out on me again—if I don't run out on you first."

"You can't forget that, Stephen? You know I didn't want to."

"You shouldn't have done it," he said coldly.

"But don't you understand why I did it?"

"I hope not," he said. "If I did, you'd be sorry."

"But I couldn't stand any more, Stephen. I couldn't go on stealing and lying—"

"What made you think you had to? Didn't you believe me when I told you all I wanted was enough so I could write, that all of what you found so distasteful was simply a means to an end?"

"I don't know," she said in a small guilty voice.

She could tell by the way his very shadow moved that he was angry. She desperately searched for some means to appease him. If he went out of here like this now she would never see him again.

"Stephen, Stephen. Don't be like that."

"Like what?" His voice was like the blade of a knife.

"Darling," she said. "Let's never fight again. Let's live the good life together, like you used to say in Chicago."

He gave a bitter, derogatory spurt of laughter. "On what?" he asked. "Your precious family's money?"

"I'll have my own money in two years," she said. "And I make quite a lot now."

"Oh, sure," he said sarcastically. "Seventy-five dollars a week is a princely sum."

"I make more than that," she said.

"I don't give a damn what you make," he spat at her. "This whole conversation is insane. You'll never need money; I always will. And if I take your stinking money, you'll make me pay for it— through the balls. Don't think I never realized, little Miss Potts, that you had a sockful of jack stashed away all along. Why didn't you part with some of your filthy lucre when we all needed it? No, instead, you, the typical preacher's daughter, preferred to steal—it didn't make any difference anyway. You'd already been baptized— thoroughly saved. Protestants!" he said in vehement fury. "How I hate the God damned Protestants!"

"I hate them too," she said weakly. Her mind ached with confusion, was dazzled with terror as if he stood over her like an avenging angel with a sword. But he wouldn't kill her; he would do something worse: he would leave her. "What can I do?" she beseeched him.

"Nobody can do anything," he said, his voice black with despair.

He was fully dressed now, even to his overcoat, and he came

over to the bed and gave her a kiss as light and cold as a snowflake. "Good-bye, kiddo."

"Stephen, Stephen!" she cried. He didn't pause.

"When will you be back?" she wailed.

"I won't be," he said at the bedroom door.

"Wait, wait," she called.

For some miraculous reason he did.

She scrambled from the bed and flew to him, holding on to his overcoat sleeves, gripping him as terror had gripped her. He laid a hand on her head. "Cheer up," he said. "You know I won't run out on you. I'm in love with you, you moron."

"Oh, Stephen," she gasped and put up her face to his, tears spilling down again.

He slightly averted his face, so that her lips did not make contact with his mouth. "I've got to think," he said. "I've got to make plans."

"For us?" she cried eagerly, not quite daring to hope. "Yup. For thou and moi. Maybe I can get a job on a newspaper. Some high-class rag like the *Enquirer*."

"Oh, Stephen, I know what that is. Don't joke."

"I'm not joking. I'm serious. I've got to make some jack and pronto. This will kill you, but I've even been locked out of my digs. I've got one buck to my name. I came up here tonight to put the bite on Gloria."

"Darling, you can put the bite on me. Any time. You know that." She went over to her chest of drawers and opened her purse. But she couldn't see what she was doing. "Turn on the light, darling," she said, "so I can see how much cash I have."

He turned on the light and though he did nothing so obvious as come over and watch over her shoulder, he did look on with interest as she went through her wallet.

The examination, he noticed, with a sinking feeling, had taken on a hurried quality, and a frown of puzzlement was on her face. She now opened a drawer and furiously began to push around things inside, searching.

"I can't find that hundred dollar bill Daddy sent me!" she exclaimed. "I thought I put it right in my wallet with my other money."

He made no comment, did nothing to distract her in her search. He hardly breathed for fear he would upset some kind of delicate balance of chance.

"I just can't find it," she said at last, pushing back a strand of birch-colored hair that had fallen in her face. She looked perplexed and distraught.

He made a small empty gesture, a wistful smile on his face. "I'm sorry, darling. I can't tell you how sorry," she said mournfully. "I have my carfare and that's all. That hundred dollar bill has just vanished."

He considered this for a moment, then said, "I think my hotel would cash a check."

"But I haven't a sou in the bank either!" she cried unhappily. "It's all in my savings account. I forgot to put any in the checking one. I'll get some out the first thing Monday morning. Can't you tell your hotel that you'll pay them in full on Monday?"

Stephen was tempted to comment sharply on her naiveté, but she was being sweet with him even if a little simple-minded. Also, he wondered what made her think a hundred would do him, though of course it would help. Anything would. "I'll try to think of some way to stall them," he told her. He saw no need to tell her that it had not been his intention to spend the night in the hotel in any case. Apple was probably searching all over the Village for him this minute.

He patted her cheek and told her she was a darling, and to get back in bed before he froze. But she insisted on walking arm in arm to the door with him.

"What will you do about food tomorrow?" she asked in concern.

"Scrounge," he grinned.

"But I want you to have a real Christmas dinner," she said.

"I'll have a real Christmas dinner some other year."

"No, wait," she said. "I've had a brainstorm. Gloria may have something in one of her purses."

Ellen went into Gloria's bedroom, leaving the door open. "You mean Gloria has so much cash these days that she can't lug it around?"

He grinned happily at Ellen's silvery answering laugh. "Victor's rich and he's generous," she said.

Stephen waited for her, feeling a small twinge of excited hope again. How much? Probably a twenty. Better than nothing. He began to pace around the room nervously. He hoped to God she'd find that much at least. Then he could take Apple out for a drink, soften her up.

He came to a stop at the mantlepiece and looked at the display of Christmas cards on top. His lip curled in derision. Bourgeois beasts, both of them. He disarranged the collection carelessly, picking up this one and that, reading the message and the signature. Most of them were, he gathered, Southern in origin. Nothing but a conservative bunch of church pillars would ever be guilty of such bad taste. They still were under the illusion that Christmas was a sacred event, to be observed solemnly, humorlessly. Then he came to a stack of unmailed Christmas cards, also unsealed. He looked at their addresses: all to men, he noticed, and without street addresses. He poked a finger inside, curiously, and a ten dollar bill fell out. He left it on the floor while he withdrew the card itself and read the message. "Merry Christmas," it said, "from Ellen Potts and Gloria Wayne."

With a little grimace he put the card back in the envelope, but he did not pick up the fallen bill. Instead, he peeked inside the other cards. All held a crisp ten dollar bill, and all were undoubtedly signed the same way. Loot for the help. All those liveried bastards downstairs trying to look busy running elevators and spying on the tenants.

He was counting the ten-card stack again when he looked up and saw Ellen. She had a twenty dollar bill in her hand. "I found this at least," she was saying before she broke off, suddenly speechless when she realized what he was doing.

Then to her amazement, she saw him give her a quizzical look and begin to pocket the envelopes. "I need this more than they do," he said with satisfaction, patting his full pocket. He didn't see the startled expression on her face, having taken for granted that she was agreeable to this method of solving his problem.

"You can't do that!" she exclaimed and made a move toward his pocket.

He grabbed her hand and forcefully drew it away from him. "Why?" he asked, his voice as steely as his grasp. His eyes were narrowed at her, but she could see that they were lightning bright with anger. He was hurting her hand.

"You just can't, that's all!" She tried to take her hand away. "It's not yours."

His other hand shot out, and open-palmed he struck her across the face. "You'd rather give it to your lackeys, huh?"

"No, Stephen!" she shook her head frantically, backing away from him, but he continued to stalk her.

"I'll break your God damned neck," he promised between his teeth. "This time I'll really do it. Stingy, ugly, sniveling little slut. Love!" He hit her again, another sharp cracking blow, this time across the nose. Immediately blood poured from it. She staggered away from him, panting, her hands trembling as she reached up to feel her face. She began to cry when she found the blood. Even in his fury he was interested to note that her great sobs literally sounded like "boo-hoo-boo." He hadn't known that people really made noises like that. Then he caught her by the throat. She screamed and struggled against him like a house cat, wrenching, clawing, squirming, her body rigid.

Her resistance sent another bolt of anger through him. The little fool was afraid of him! She didn't trust him. She thought he was really going to hurt her! All right, he would hurt her. He'd teach her to think he was capable of insane violence. He half dragged her around the room, then he spied the corner of the mantlepiece. An excellent place to crack her head open. He drew back the taut neck, grinned into her wide-eyed terrified face, repulsively messy, unkempt and unattractive with all that blood. Some of it was even matting her hair. "No, Stephen, no!" she was trying to say, but he put his hand over her mouth tightly, so she couldn't bite.

"This is for your generosity," he said and slammed her head again and again against the mantlepiece.

When she went limp and fell to the floor he thought she was dead. She looked dead. He touched her with a foot. She reminded him of a canary he had once massacred pour le sport at the age of ten. It had been his mother's canary. Yellow and small and pathetic. All bloody. Completely changed from the way it had been. He felt a terrible surge of longing. Tender broken bird. So pretty before. The least he could do was clean her up. It was wrong to make things ugly and messy, disorder was so unpleasant. He touched the head of the broken bird. Tiny sweet little head. He remembered its shrill little voice. So sweet and happily it sang.

The head stirred under his hand. The eyes opened. They didn't look like the eyes of anyone he knew. Why were they so full, so glassy. They didn't even look human. Thoughtfully, he touched the blood at the edge of the open mouth. Under his hand, he could feel the warmth of breath. The mouth was moving, trying to say something. He leaned closer. "Victor's money," the mouth gasped. "A loan—"

Stephen stood up, looking uncomprehendingly at the moving mouth. "Alone," it was saying.

It was eerie.

"Victor made me a loan," the orifice said again.

Even after he left the building, having hidden his own messy condition as best as he could under his blood-stained coat, he wasn't sure what the mouth had meant. We are all alone, he muttered philosophically to himself, and let it go at that.

XX

"I don't give one durn who Titter Terrill and them is entertainin' tonight!" Frank Otha Potts raged through his wife's lovely Southern ancestral home. "YOU CAIN'T GO!"

"Shh, shh," Ellen heard her mother's voice. "What on earth are you trying to do? Wake up Ellen T.T.? Peenie didn't say she was going; she just said she'd like to go. And I don't blame her the least little bit. After all, the child hasn't been hardly anywhere, and this is New Year's Eve—"

"Aaaah—" came Frank Pott's expression of disgust, a sagging, expiring sound like the air being let out of a giant balloon.

Ellen waited for more, her consciousness alertly arched toward the ruckus in the drawing room which had indeed awakened her, but she heard nothing. She crawled from her bed, as stealthy as a sneak thief, and peered down the hall. Her sister Peenie (short for Peanut which is what Ellen had declared she looked like when she was born, though the name she was registered under at Gunston Hall was Mary India Tate Potts) was gulping and bawling out her grief and disappointment at the head of the staircase, having converted the newel post into a small wailing wall. Ellen discreetly withdrew. That Frank really was a tyrannical bastard.

Though fully awake now, she crawled back in bed, doing so gently to favor her bruises. They all expected her to stay in bed for officially she was still sick. Ellen, and the rest of them too, realized that she was nothing of the kind; but since a miracle had clearly saved her the least she could do by way of gratitude was remain convalescent for a decent period. To stave off impatience she therefore slept a great deal. When she didn't sleep she found that she spent her time in worrying—about everything. Which began with the way she looked.

Now, automatically, she reached for her hand mirror on the night table; she consulted it far oftener than was necessary to see how she was getting along. Her face was fixed in cold disapproval as she brought the mirror up to it, but she knew it really wasn't so bad. With dark glasses she could even go out. The black and blue discolorations and puffiness under the eyes were receding nicely; she no longer looked like a blonde raccoon. But she touched the broken nose—the cause of the bruises—very gingerly. Maybe they should have set it though they had insisted in Doctors' Hospital in New York that it wasn't that sort of break; that once the swelling and sensitivity left it her nose would be as good as ever. She put back the mirror with a sigh. All of it could have been so much, they said, worse. Could it, she wondered, could it really? Perhaps from their point of view. Except for the headaches, resulting from the concussion which logically should have been a skull fracture, the nose, and the various aches and hideous bruises, she had no physical souvenirs; in a few days even these would be gone. And that would be the time to bail out.

The thought shot through her like a strong stimulant, and the pain in her head began to pulse again. New York—it excited and frightened her, as if she were a prisoner planning a jail break. When could she do it? Could she do it? How? Everyone here naturally assumed that after her awful experience she would have learned her lesson and would have sense enough to stay put. She touched her nose again thoughtfully. Thank God he hadn't disfigured her for life. Would Sissy really try to make them keep her part open for her? What would she do if they didn't? For she had an awful feeling she was going to need the money. This because the cat was out of the bag, thanks to Walter and/or Courtney. Not all out yet, but forepaws and whiskers: her daddy knew she had been on the wicked stage. Walter had worsened, not amended, by appealing to her father's reason. Since that time he had simply not believed a word Ellen said, including her account of the tragedy.

At seven A.M. on Christmas day Ellen had come to, finding herself on the floor where Stephen had left her, and she had crawled to the telephone not knowing the time, and hardly the day, but trembling and crying with hysterical self-pity, vaguely aware that the apartment was as still and cold as fallen snow which meant she was all alone. Her intention had been to telephone downstairs for help, but the phone had obliged her by ringing just as she reached it.

"Merry Christmas!" Courtney's bright merry Christmas voice had greeted her. "We're just off for the airport and hoped we'd reach you before you went to Connecticut."

From then on the plans of the Charlesworths also took a drastic change. They hurried right over with their own doctor and the ambulance followed. She was rushed to Doctors' Hospital, thoroughly examined, X-rayed, questioned, and, at Walter's vehement insistence, dismissed. He contended that she was better off at home with her own folks to take care of her, since there wasn't a great deal wrong, than staying on in New York alone and friendless, though hospitalized, for a few days' observation. Twelve hours later—at seven P.M.—they were on the plane.

Feeling and looking more like a basket case than a happy Christmas surprise (she now had two black eyes and enough good-sized lumps on her head to make her resemble the business end of a caveman's club), she was nonetheless given the normal Charlesworth treatment, though they let her have an hour's nap after take-off. Walter, as businesslike as an attorney, submitted his findings. He had talked to the doorman and elevator men on duty when the burglar had come in; it appeared that he was no stranger to the house even if he was, as Ellen had said, "no friend of hers." It appeared that he was at least an acquaintance of Ellen's roommate, Miss Wayne; that though his name was not known several times he had called on her—late at night—and that on at least two occasions she had been known to meet him in the lobby and hand him an envelope, presumably containing money. What did Ellen know about this? Nothing. Had this Gloria person never mentioned him? Never. Where had she been all night anyway? Out. Well— she certainly did not sound like the sort of girl they would think Ellen's parents would consider a suitable roommate, or a good influence, for that matter, if she knew such characters…. Ellen had nothing to say. Nor did she have anything to say when Walter informed her that he intended to keep telephoning until he found Miss Wayne in, so they could find out just who this person was. He was sure Ellen's daddy would call in the F.B.I. and even the president, if necessary, to get to the bottom of this terrible crime. With this Ellen listlessly agreed. The thief would be punished, for he had not stolen just her money, but had tried to steal her life.

Ellen had nodded gravely, only too appreciative of just how true this really was. But she had no more intention at that moment of turning Stephen in than she had the day they had left Chicago, when Stephen had started stealing her life; the brutality and robbery of money had been a simple culmination. And an unnecessary one. Her own thoughtlessness and self-absorption were responsible. Why hadn't she thought of giving Stephen the Christmas tip money in the first place? True, Victor had loaned it to her—her half—but only because in the last-minute rush of Christmas shopping she had run short of cash because she had not gone to the bank. Only technically had it been Victor's money. She was to have paid him back on Monday. How cruel and how vicious to have taunted Stephen with a promise of money when he needed it so desperately, then to offer him a twenty dollar bill when he had discovered that she could have made it a hundred! No, in his estimation (and who could blame him for it), she had unconsciously rated him lower than a servant. And if this discovery had driven him into savage madness which could only be cured by bloodshed, was it his fault?

Wherever he was, poor darling, she wished him well. And she could think poor darling dispassionately. For he had not killed her on Christmas Eve; he had killed himself, had ended his own mythical being for her once and for all. Before the dramatic climax there had been so many things; and today, being X-rayed, tapped, prodded, observed as scientifically as if she were a mere thing under a microscope, had left her free to find her own Christmas gift to herself—freedom. Now, wherever he was, and she had an idea he would not seek the proximate and therefore dangerous haven of Apple Ashby, but would sensibly go far, far away, she wished him well and surcease; maybe he could walk the cancer out of his system; maybe he could trade personalities with a bear; maybe he would meet a rattler willing to draw Stephen's venom out, adding it to its own, for a price. Godspeed him with his pathetic hundred dollars!

And thus had she thought as they landed at the Charlotte airport, where they were met by her frantic and outraged daddy who had been telephoned ahead and had, typically, rushed there with an ambulance and a police escort for speed.

XXI

Aside from release of love for Stephen, Ellen had received another Christmas bonus, thus far no one had been able to locate Gloria Wayne, and it was not from lack of trying. Which made this a bonus indeed.

Every day, Ellen knew, her father zealously called the number of their New York apartment, and each day he contacted the manager of their telephone exchange; he had directed them to refer, until further notice, all calls, be they wrong numbers or the laundryman, collect, to Miss Potts here in Crump, North Carolina. He had also called the New York Bureau of Missing Persons, and of course the renting agents for their apartment, and God knows who else. He was a thorough man. If Miss Gloria Wayne existed, he said, he would find her.

Ellen's awe at her father's determination was nothing compared to her admiration at Gloria's ability to elude him. She had no idea where Gloria was, but wherever she was, Ellen hoped she would understand. Ellen's guilt at having inadvertently implicated Gloria, to whom, in accepting her after the breakup of the triumvirate, she had extended a supererogatory loyalty, was still as sore as a thumb. And when Frank Potts beseeched Ellen to pray for guidance, she did so fervently. She asked the Dear Lord to tell her where Gloria was, how she was, and how she had managed to stay impervious to all this. So far her prayers had not been answered, but she had a strong feeling that Gloria Knew All, and had somehow worked it out.

Ellen stretched back in her bed, miserable and sleepless, and closed her eyes. When she opened them, she knew, the same old remembrances of things past would be there: her holy virgin years—the keepsakes. of Sweet Briar which were the latest additions made to the room. It contained mementos of all of her selves from eight to eighteen, but nothing after. Her present self was enclosed in a hard opaque case; there was nothing exposed to shed itself upon the girlish sweetness and trust of this adolescent bower.

"You asleep, Ellen T.T.?" Peenie asked from the door. "No," she said for herself. "You're not," and she came into her sister's room, firmly shutting the door behind her in such a way as to indicate that she had a confidence to make.

Ellen yawned, asked her the time, and sat up in bed, preparing herself for receipt of Peenie's secret.

"Nadine says supper's about ready," Peenie said, sitting down close beside her on the edge of the bed. "And Daddy says you're to get dressed and come down for it."

Ellen took this news with considerable surprise. "Why?"

Peenie didn't know why, except maybe because Mama had invited Cousin Walter and Courtney over for it. "And he said it was high time you stopped nursing those black eyes, and anyway you're the only one yankeefied enough to be able to talk to yankees."

Ellen shook her head. "He certainly is mean today," she commented. "Do you reckon he's planning for me to go to the midnight services tonight with you all?"

"I don't know what he's planning," Peenie said bitterly.

Ellen smiled. "I heard all that commotion about your going to Titter's."

"Don't worry," said Peenie. "I'm going. If it harelips hell." Ellen looked at her sister thoughtfully, considering her Peenie's practically open rebellion. Ellen and her brother F.O., Jr. had preferred the underground variety. But then she and her brother had been "wanted," and Peenie had just come along, dropped in her parent's laps like a peanut falling from the balcony at the picture show. "What kind of party's Titter having?" Ellen inquired.

"Probably marvelous," Peenie told her. "Why don't you come?"

"What? Looking like this?" Ellen laughed, but knew her looks had nothing to do with it. Titter's party would be, like all parties this season and any other in Crump, North Carolina, just a kid party for Ellen. She couldn't imagine herself ever again being thus entertained.

"Just put on your dark glasses, sweetie, and I'll lend you a long dress if you didn't bring one."

While Ellen was trying to visualize herself thus, which was as far as she was willing to go with the experiment, Peenie spoke again, but on another subject. "I'm going to fix Daddy tonight," she promised.

Ellen glanced at her quickly, the hatred in Peenie's voice startling and strong. She saw that Peenie's face was almost transformed by what she was feeling.

"—Making fools out of us all those years," Peenie muttered. "Everything him, him, him—never anything we wanted to do, not even now. What good's his old money to us. God!" Peenie exclaimed. "How sorry I do feel for that baby upstairs!"

Ellen knew precisely what Peenie meant, and she couldn't blame her. But still, Ellen having been one of the favored, she couldn't share his sister's feeling, though all the money sometimes made Ellen feel sick, and the things that had been done to get it made her feel sicker. The local wags called their father a Protestant Jesuit, and the poor boxes generously distributed throughout his tabernacle were known as "Potts boxes." Ellen knew that of the three children it was Peenie who most resented having been dressed, as they were each Sunday in childhood, in white cheesecloth and gilded cardboard wings and mounted on the platform to sing in their shrill angel voices. The money had rolled in from these siren songs, and Ellen agreed with Peenie that the latest addition to their family—Milton, aged two—had been made in the hope of helping their father achieve another bonanza.

"You can't change Daddy now," Ellen said in such a mild voice that she immediately regretted it. And sure enough, it got Peenie's back even further up.

"You just wait and see what I do to 'change him'!" Peenie cried, glaring at her. "He's not the only Potts on earth! I'm as much Potts as he isI I can be just as vulgar and sneaky and common—"

"Good Lord, Peeniel" Ellen suddenly exclaimed in vast amusement. The whole thing was really ludicrous. "Now, come on. What can you do to 'fix him,' as you call it?"

"Get him drunk."

Ellen's smile broadened. People had always said Peenie was a genius. "You crazy thing! How, Peenie? What are you going to do? Spike his buttermilk?"

"Okay. Break up. Roll on the floor if you think it's so funny."

"It is funny. It's a scream. But how, you little devil?"

"Just wait and see."

"I will," said Ellen, eager now to get out of bed and get dressed. She grabbed up her robe. On her way to the bath she gave Peenie an admiring look and a silent vote of confidence. Peenie, she was glad to see, seemed somewhat relaxed, and rather pleased with herself, now that she had talked over her plans.

"I'm going downstairs," Peenie called. "But hurry, if you don't want to miss anything."

"You mean watching you get Daddy drunk?" Ellen called back rather gaily.

Peenie came to the bathroom door and grinned at Ellen. "He'll be so skonked when he gets up there on that platform tonight to strut his stuff that he'll break his fool neck."

After her bath Ellen came out and started getting dressed She felt a little shaky, but more excited than ill. She dressed, however, slowly, tenderly touching her bruised spots as she did so, as if they were pets.

It was the first time she had a dress on in a week, and the mirror told her she was positively emaciated. She hated to be seen by anybody—even the cousins. And if her father did expect her to come to his New Year's Eve services? But of course she would go. She always had. This was her daddy's big night every year. Even her mother attended at New Year's, though she steadfastly refused even at this time to answer to the name of "Sister Potts," if so addressed.

New Year's Eve was the culmination of Frank Potts' annual crusade—a perfectly valid name, historically speaking, for his going on the spiritual warpath. It was also the anniversary of his "seeing the light and getting the call." The first miracle, which had occurred twelve years before on New Year's eve, had put a stop to his faithless, wastrel libidinous life. In, that sacred year of discovery he had balked at the seasonal punch bowl like a horse at a rattle snake and had never touched a drop since. A formidable record, and now about to be broken, if Peenie had her way.

Fleetingly, she wondered again exactly what Peenie was planning, touched perfume to her ears, picked up her dark glasses from the dresser and fitted them over her blackened eyes. She was ready for the descent.

## XXII

The sounds of the gathering, mingled with the good smells of Nadine's cooking, curled up to Ellen as she went down the stairway. For the first time since she had arrived, she felt she was back home again. Everything shone with high polish. It was all rather beautiful and bright and glad. She heard a shriek of laughter. Milton, the baby; then her father's booming joviality, like distant thunder, and the answering broadsides of Walter's and F.O.'s. It sounded very gay; a real houseful. They were all talking at once, of course.

She followed the noise and came to the library door where she paused, actress-like, receiving the "Well, *Ellen*!" and "Doesn't she look fine!" and the oohs and ahhs she expected. Milton came and grabbed her around the legs and tried to pick her up. She almost fell, and giggling rather hysterically, was helped to right herself by her older brother. She beamed at them and they beamed at her, and had she not known better, she would have sworn that the drinks they held in their hands were cocktails. However, her mother whose voice was almost as clear and lilting as Ellen's own, said, "Which will you have, Sister, tomato juice or grape?"

"Grape," said Ellen and received her cocktail from her brother.

"Frank, I'll say this," Walter announced. "You've got a mighty good-looking family. Of course most of it comes from Leta's side." He gave Ellen a broad wink.

"Piffle," said her father and threw an arm around Ellen. "Ellen's the looker in the bunch and she's the image of me." Everyone laughed at this, for nothing could have been less true. Ellen looked like the Tates, while both Peenie and F.O. looked like Pottses through and through. They were stoutly made, though Peenie's frame would not absolutely assert this for some years yet, but both had Frank's hair, his vivid cerulean eyes, and his knobby pug nose. But, as Walter had said, they were all good-looking. Peenie's hair had been enhanced since she'd been away at school by a red rinse. She wore it in a pageboy cut and it shone like a copper bell. Ellen really thought she was the prettiest of them all, including their delicate, regal-looking mother.

Ellen grinned and sipped her grape juice, then caught Peenie's eye. Peenie was trying, eye-language, to tell her something. Ellen glanced down at her own glass and understood. There was definitely something in it. She tasted it again. Vodka. She looked up at her father, who still clasped her, and holding her own breath, gave him an ecstatic smile. He squeezed her. "My little girl's thin," he said, and a nice fume of vodka breath rolled out with the words. Ellen smiled and thought: that devil Peenie!

Nadine, the Negro cook, smiled at her people as she passed down the hall and in a few minutes Buck, her husband, and their houseboy, came in and told them supper was served. They all trouped out of the library toward the dining room, leaving their fruit juice glasses behind.

Ellen's arm was captured by Courtney who whispered, "Did you taste something in your drink?" and then when she thought Frank was listening, said in a loud voice, "Leta, I think that's about the prettiest Christmas tree I ever saw."

"F.O., Jr. picked it," said Leta, as F.O., Jr. helped her be seated in her chair at the head of the table. "He and Frank and Buck went out to the woods and chopped it. It took all three of them, didn't it, Son? it was so big."

"I'll declare it is big," Courtney said rather breathlessly as with

Frank's assistance she settled herself in her seat.

"Ain't it awful hot in here?" Frank asked at large.

"Get Buck to open a window," Leta said. "It is warm." Ellen thought she saw a ghost of a smile pass between her brother and Peenie. She then looked at her father's face. It was always what you might call florid, but tonight it was glowing like a Halloween lantern. However, she decided, the vodka would wear off during dinner.

"This dad-burned heat's enough to roast a chicken," Ellen's father complained, and pushing back from his chair went to raise a window himself. He staggered slightly as he reached it, causing an audible snicker from Peenie, then threw up the sash and cried, "Whew! That's better!" as the air rushed in. He returned to the table, and in chill and silence they began to eat their soup. Ellen ventured another look in demure Peenie's direction, but Peenie, apparently satisfied with her results so far, was strictly attending to the matter of feeding herself.

"Well, F.O., Jr.," said Courtney brightly. "Leta tells me you're a big football star this year."

And in relief Ellen watched the conversation gallop off to the field of sports. Next came the matter of fraternities (F.O., Jr. was a Phi Garn pledge) and colleges in general, followed by the inevitable subject of integration in the South. Here, Frank Potts roared in, as he had heavy States' Rights opinions on this issue even if he had none on colleges and fraternities, never having been a college man himself.

"Daddy, you make me sick," Peenie said at one point, after her father had deliberately ignored Leta's warning looks toward the kitchen, indicating that Nadine and Buck might overhear.

Frank Potts held a buttered biscuit in one large paw. He glared at his youngest daughter, his hand working over the biscuit as if it were a yo-yo. Then he slammed it down, rose, his napkin falling away from his vest, "Durn your little hide!" You talk just like a yankee. You and Ellen!"

"Frank, Frank," Leta tried to calm him. "Don't get so worked up. Peenie didn't mean anything by it."

But he had strode menacingly around to Peenie's place.

"Make you sick, huh?" He grabbed her by her silky red hair. "Leave the table. THIS MINUTE!" And he jerked her to her feet and gave her a push out of the dining room. "Anybody else want to leave? How about you, Miss Broadway Star?"

Everyone, white-faced and silent, turned to look at Ellen, his new victim. "Sit down, Daddy," she said quietly.

"I'll smack your God damn mouth off!" was his reply, and with that, his face brutal with rage, he left the dining room too.

The others sat, stricken, unmoving, and from the direction of the stairs they heard a loud bellow followed by a sharp crack. Then screaming.

"Has he lost his mind?" Courtney asked as if to himself.

"You want me to go see?" Walter asked Leta, half rising.

"I'll go," Leta said and slipped from her place.

Ellen tried to restore her calm and lifted her soup spoon, but her hand was shaking. She put it down and said nothing.

"I never heard Daddy curse like that," F.O. commented tonelessly.

"Do you think he struck Peenie?" Courtney ventured to ask. "Maybe you had better go see, Walter. He might harm both of them."

Walter seemed to think about it, but did not stir. All four of them sat there quietly, consumed in thought. Upstairs they could hear the baby crying, then rapid footsteps as Nadine went up the back stairs to quiet him. Frank's uproar had apparently awakened him. But there were no more cracks of blows being delivered, nor were there any murmurs. If Leta and Frank were having a conversation, it was a private one, somewhere behind closed doors.

"Peenie's little prank certainly backfired," Walter announced finally.

"I could have told her it would," Courtney said, the authority on alcohol. "Frank Potts always did lose his temper when he was drinking—just one little drop—"

"Hush, Sister," her husband told her.

"I'm sorry. I apologize," Courtney said, and Ellen murmured that it was quite all right. But her brother was rudely offended. He arose from the table and excused himself.

"I truly am sorry," Courtney apologized again, this time directly to Ellen.

Ellen shook her head. "I hope Mama gets him to sleep before it's time to go to the service."

"Lord, so do I!" Courtney agreed.

Then all three looked up in surprise as Leta and a very abashed Peenie, her face cherubic and fresh washed from tears making her into a little girl again now that her makeup was gone, came back into the dining room. They took their places once more, and Walter hopped up at the last minute to help Leta be seated.

Leta's composure, false though it was, reassured them. She rang for Nadine who came and cleared the soup plates as if she were clearing mere soup plates, not wreckage. Then while they waited for the next course, Leta remarked that she had heard today that Sara Sue Blackburn was going up to Washington and testify against the "Twenty-One" show, on which she had failed to win a penny in the horse-racing category.

With lively relief, Walter and Courtney—especially Courtney whose fifth cousin Sara Sue was—dived for the diversion and happily emersed themselves in it.

Ellen listened to the frolicking and splashing of this conversation and wondered where her father was. She glanced at Peenie, but Peenie, unrepentant looking and sour-faced, did not glance back. Ellen also wondered what had happened to her brother. Altogether she wondered about the whole thing. Her father's notorious temper had been lost and found many times before—at table, on the lawn, in the pulpit, parlor, bedroom and bath. But he seldom went around hitting people, and certainly he never "took the Lord's name in vain," having confined himself, since his reformation, to those euphemistic expletives dear to the Bible Belter's heart: Shoot! Durn! Hell-ena, Montana!

And thus the meal passed.

After dinner, Courtney and Walter thanked Leta effusively and left; they had a party to go to before they attended Frank's midnight worship.

As soon as they had gone, F.O. came out of hiding, but not so his father. He stood uncertainly in the drawing room to which the ladies had withdrawn, and looked at his mother strangely while she chattered to the company at large. "Peenie, do go call Mrs. Duckworth for me, will you?" she asked. "Tell her that fruit cake we sent to Cousin Mary Starr never did get there and she'll have to put a tracer on it."

"Why can't we do it tomorrow?" Peenie asked sulkily. "Who's going to be worrying about fruit cakes on New Year's Eve?"

"Now do go, dear, while I'm thinking about it. Ellen, do you really feel up to going out? I'm sure your daddy will forgive you this once. I do hope Milton's not going to be awake half the night. F.O., honey, see if you can adjust that lamp over there and make it stop flickering. Didn't you say you had some studying to do for that make-up exam?"

"I must say this is one fine way to spend New Year's Eve," Peenie said sullenly, as she went out into the hall to telephone. She had, Ellen gathered, completely discarded the idea of going over to Titter's. Maybe that was what the smack had been about; it was just like her to have defied their father in that particular moment and told him her plans. But where was he? Ellen asked her mother.

"Daddy's having a nap," Leta said. "On the library couch."

Her mother's face was as serene and bland as a Southern sky; her disposition apparently unblemished by the ugly scene her husband had made. Ellen marveled at her, as she always did, after such skirmishes. All of her mother's fussiness and nerves were dissolved by attention to harmless details. "What was wrong with Daddy?" she asked, phrasing the question cautiously.

"Indigestion, I expect," her mother lied as lightly and gracefully as a flutter of a hand. "He had a great big helping of cobbler at lunch. Then he's been upset, Ellen," she said meaningfully. "We've all been so concerned about you. Are you sure you're feeling yourself again? Daddy and I were talking it over: we think it would be nice if you finished out the year some place not so far away, so you could come home on week-ends."

"I don't particularly want to go back to college," Ellen said. "You know that. I told you so. Besides, it's harder to get into schools than you think."

Her mother made a gesture, indicating that this was no problem, that Frank Potts could fix anything. F.O. looked up sharply from his occupation with the lamp to see what his sister would say. Ellen, a brooding expression on her face, said nothing. She sat in her chair and stared at the floor; the filial tug was as strong as an undertow, and as it pulled at her, her inner identity as Ellen Tate Terrill Potts seemed to slough away like encrusted layers of skin. She could remember vaguely having wanted in New York to become a woman, but here she was a child. Her mother's face, reflecting Ellen as if it were a mirror, said so.

"Ellen's grown up," she heard her, brother say. "She's been

living her own life."

"If this is the case," Leta said quietly, "I think Ellen would be the first to agree that she's not doing so well with it—and isn't really ready to. Remember, son, we could have lost Ellen."

Lost Ellen. That, thought Ellen, should have been my name. She got up. "I think I'll go rest awhile," she said tiredly.

Her mother told her she thought this was a good idea, and Ellen could feel both of them watching her as she left the room. She found Peenie sitting listlessly in the hall by the phone.

"Well?" asked Ellen.

"Well nothing," Peenie replied.

"It was vodka, wasn't it?" Ellen asked.

"No, it was gin. Nadine's. But it certainly worked. Go look in the library."

Ellen raised her eyes in a question, but tiptoed down the hall and peeped in the library door. Her father had his back to her, but he seemed to sense she was there. He lurched around, stared a moment, then gave her a loose-lipped broad smile. His eyes stood as still as a stopped clock. They were slightly crossed. He lumbered away from the desk, a water tumbler in his hand. Ellen saw the bottle of medicinal brandy, a half-pint bottle, lying empty on the couch. Frank Potts leaned heavily against the book shelves and called, "Come in, daughter. Let's have a little talk!"

<h1 style="text-align:center">XXIII</h1>

The doormen exchanged glances as they helped Miss Wayne out of the taxi. It was the first time they had seen her in a week and she looked awful. She managed a weak smile and tried to walk to the lobby on her own, but it was clear to them that they'd better stand by. One hovered by her elbow while the other quickly opened the plate glass door. The burst of hot air upon entering made her stagger a little, and over her head the two men again visually consulted each other: was she that drunk? Already? New Year's Eve or not, it was only nine o'clock.

One of the doormen tried to get into the elevator with her, but she shook her head. "I'm all right, Pat. Don't bother to go up with me."

But she certainly didn't look all right. And once she got upstairs she certainly wouldn't find that things were all right, unless she already knew. "Miss Potts has gone," said Pat.

Gloria nodded, "Yes, I know," she said lifelessly, and the elevator door closed.

Gloria, holding herself taut against the back of the elevator, the only way she was comfortable with all the mending ribs, waited with her eyes closed until they reached her floor. The aching agony was gone, had been gone for a day or so, but she was soggy with fatigue and the remembrance of pain. All kinds. She didn't know where to begin. But it really all began with Stephen on Christmas eve.

She and Victor had made a sentimental journey to the Village after dining at the Four Seasons with some friends of his; and they had gone, of course, back to the old stomping grounds where they had met that first night. And that's where Stephen came in. She wished she could remember it more clearly. All of them had been high, and singing their heads off, by the time Stephen arrived. And she had continued to sing, Victor urging her on, telling everyone how she used to be with a jazz band in Chi. Stephen, with that bookshop girl of his, had joined them, she remembered, looking very sober and very bored. She had never met Apple before and never wanted to again. Apple, as she recalled, had been vulgar, stiff and insulting. Gloria couldn't even remember when Apple left. Then there had been more of the same.

"This is your floor, Miss Wayne," she heard the elevator man saying, and she stumbled out of the door, knowing he would wait and watch until she put her key in the lock.

She accomplished this and heard the elevator's faint whirr as it went away. Inside the door was the week's accumulation of mail. She stepped over it and walked to the nearest lamp, switched it on, then immediately went to the telephone. She dialed Victor's number again, and again got the shrill female voice asking, who is it? and hung up. Then she cried, silently, the tears gushing down her face like a hot geyser, wetting her hands which supported her head, dripping onto the soiled material of her once-best dress. She got up and poured herself a large Scotch.

I should call Ellen and get it over with, she thought. But she just sat. Will he put the money in the bank? she wondered. Was I right to have given Steve all that cash? Suppose he has no intention of putting the money in the bank? I'll know day after tomorrow, she told herself, and meantime I mustn't cough. But no wonder she had this cold. How had she ended up sleeping on a park bench in Washington Square anyway? Listlessly, her ribs hurting again, Gloria looked around the empty room. She glanced at the Christmas cards on the mantle. Christmas was over and done. "Merry

Christmas," she whispered to herself. The sound was hollow as an ancient tomb. All of it had come and gone.

Her eyes continued their vacant travels, the expression on her face longing, the skin drawn. There was no life in the room. How much would all this junk bring? Who cared? She ached as if she were hungry, but it was only the broken ribs. Thank God, at least, Steve had broken the bastard's nose. Or had he? All she remembered was that by that time she knew the whole story with Ellen, that they both knew Ellen had been dismissed from the hospital and had gone off with relatives, and then just before Stephen hit the son-of-a-bitch he reminded her that he was an expert at breaking noses. And his blood had not run blue, as he kept saying it was, but red just like anybody else's. She didn't even know his name. All, she knew was that he kept telling her his family was first-family Boston and that he was a Harvard graduate and a member of the Porcellian Club. He had been very tall and thin and looked like a moth-eaten raven in his rusty but very correct chesterfield. He had had a kick like an ostrich; hence the broken ribs. He had meant them for Stephen, but Stephen had adroitly stepped out of the way. And Stephen had looked at her lying in all that mess of spit and cigarette butts and God knows what all on the floor by the bar stool and had said, helping her up, "Got any money? Let's pay the check and get out of here."

Whimpering aloud, a luxury of loneliness, she picked up the phone and dialed Victor's apartment again. The same voice answered, and when Gloria again did not speak, said, "I know all about you, you whore!" and banged the receiver down. But this brought no freshets from the tear ducts; apparently they had had it for the moment. Mrs. Victor Rose, Shrew but Wife, had had worse things to say in the past five days. Gloria shook her head in despair. How? Why?

She got up, holding her side, and went to the bedroom, glancing once more at the defiled Christmas greetings on the mantle. Stephen had gotten one hundred there, and how much had she given him today, an hour ago, for his "stake" out West? But at least he was gone. She lowered herself to her bed, and pulled up the satin coverlet over her. Tomorrow the maid would come. And go. No Victor, no maid. No Victor, no nothing. Why? Why? How had it all happened? She emptied her mind, as if it were a trash bucket, and stared at the wall, dark and shadowy gray in the light reflected from outside. But nothing warm and soft came to take the place of the things in her head which she had ejected. Instead, little by little, the old slime seeped back in, holding sleep at arm's length. She decided to have another drink; alcohol was the only ingredient to produce the desired emulsion. She rose painfully and went back to the living room bar and freshened her drink. Holding it, she stared with tears in her eyes at the painting on the wall. It was Victor's, had come from his office. He had bought it in Paris. I'll send it back tomorrow, she thought. I can't keep anything that is really his, since I no longer am. She looked at her arm, her hands and her fingernails. The nail polish was chipped and the nails were dirty. From rubbing Steve's oily hair, she thought. Night after night as they had lain in bed together, like, he had said, a fragment from Laocoön. Pronounced Lay-ok-oo-wan. She knew she would never be able to find it in the dictionary, for she only knew how it sounded. "Vic!" she cried aloud, rather drunk now. "Where are you?"

She sank down on the floor, holding on to the bar and cried as if she had an audience. She couldn't think. She couldn't think. She'd ask Steve why. But Steve was gone. She had given him money to go, while there was still time, he'd said. But Gloria knew Ellen would never let them do anything to him. And she was all right. The hospital people had said so. Ellen was fine. She was in the bosom of her family. In the bosom of the lamb. Down South, where the soft cotton grows. Naturally he'd thought he'd killed her. Gloria staggered to her feet to go look at the pile of mail by the door. Ellen would write, at least. She'd do that. Ellen was thoughtful, sweet, a real lady. Much better than Steve deserved. She still didn't understand why he had done it. It hadn't made any sense, but then she had not been listening. All she had known was that Victor had gone, he had thrown her away. Then they had been standing at the cashier's desk in the Sidney and she had written a check to pay his bill. Then upstairs. That was when her ribs bad started hurting. Not just a hangover. But Stephen had said he would make her forget. Only the next morning she had waked him up groaning, he had said. And that's when the doctor came and strapped her up. Just two little broken ribs. But where was Victor?

Gloria focused her eyes on the letters. Then the writing blurred again. She sat down unexpectedly, her knees suddenly giving out, and felt the impact on her tail bone. It made her smile, this hurt, as if she had outsmarted it. I'm drunk again, she thought. You can't hurt me. Not at all. No, Victor Rose Tail-bone, I'm going to be all right. She sat up, the letters falling from her hand, and, clutching a few of them, went back to the bar to replenish her drink.

Oh, ho, ho, she sang to herself, spilling Scotch out of her glass and into it, what a time we had! She turned, starry-eyed, once again to Victor's painting. You can't mean it, she toasted the picture, Victor doesn't. He'll come back. He knows Steve is an old pal; old pals have to sleep together once in a while. Anyway, darling, I wouldn't have, she thought, thinking that she spoke it, if you hadn't turned so ice cold. Imagine ditching me in a bar and going off like that with Stephen's zoftic little pal; you like 'em lean and hard. Did you have a good lay, baby? Was she fun? Gloria laughed aloud, and heard herself and stopped.

Victor had called. The Sydney. Victor had been to the apartment; Victor had found out about Ellen. Victor had said that Stephen belonged in an insane asylum. Victor had said good-bye. Victor— She staggered to the couch, looking at the telephone, wishing she had the strength to make it there. But it was no good. Victor was through. "I'll put a thousand bucks in your account," he had said. "That should compensate for your trouble." She had been sober—or semi-sober—then. It was hard to be completely drunk in the Algonquin where they had met the day after Christmas; or at least she had found it so. The place was too mellow; good only and eternally for people who came in with a buzz on and left the same way, regardless of the number of drinks they had had. She had tried to be as sober as the atmosphere, just slightly high. She had smiled and laughed, but Victor was cold. "I can't get a divorce from Rachel," he told her. "You know that. I care for you, Gloria, but I have my youngsters to consider."

She had then told him how much she loved him.

"I'll put a thousand bucks—" his words trailed off in her memory. She sobbed for a moment, then somehow got to her feet. She went to the phone and dialed his number again. This time there was no answer, so, humming to herself, she went back to her letters scattered on the floor. She picked them up as if she were gathering fallen blossoms, still humming rather insanely. She immediately threw down those that were obviously bills or advertisements, and only hesitated before discarding those pieces of mail addressed to Ellen. Then, she found, there was nothing. Not even a late Christmas card. She screwed up her eyes and cursed at the mantlepiece display. None of those were hers either. Or just two or three. She went over and dashed the whole collection to the floor. Then cried anew as she looked at them at her feet. They hadn't done her any harm. They, along with the rest of it, had meant her good: "You never meant it!" she cried aloud. "You never meant it at all!" And he hadn't. Stephen was right; had been all along. Victor had never meant it.

She gazed at her forsaken room, the tears blurring her eyes so that there seemed to be a halo around everything she looked at. Why had he said he would divorce that shrew? Why had he bought all of these things if he hadn't loved her? Love was for maniacs. Sniffling, she gathered up the fallen letters, holding her arm to her hurting side and went off to bed.

Again, in her bedroom, she found that the gray, mean light reminded her of all the things she was; of all the things that had been. The bed seemed cold; the absence of Victor by her side as evident as a corpse. This bed would never be warm and full again. She got up tiredly; she had to sleep, she had to sleep. The ball was over, and sobriety was coming up. She wandered into Ellen's empty room. Tenderly she touched Ellen's things, and she thought of Ellen. The way Stephen had described her, after he left her maimed and crushed and dirty. How can such people exist? she thought. How can Stephen and I go on? But we do.

She picked up Ellen's white bedside telephone and dialed Victor's number and waited for seven rings. She snuffled to herself waiting, as if she had an allergy. Then she put her finger on the contact bar and broke off. She shook her head and cleared her throat, and dialed the operator to ask her to put through a person-to-person call to Miss Ellen Potts in Crump, North Carolina. No, she didn't know the number.

## XXIV

Nervous as a cat, Nadine shuddered, picked up the ringing phone and growled "Hello?" into it. People should know better than to call in time of trouble. "Miss What?" she asked, putting her finger to her ear. Buck was vacuuming the hall rug where Mr. Frank had thrown up all over it. If scrubbing and brushing wouldn't remove the stain, vacuuming wouldn't either.

The operator repeated her question once more, and Nadine, doubly resenting her clipped yankee voice, full of exasperation, raised her own, "I heah you! Ain't no need for you to shout at me! I'll see if she's in!"

Indicating to Buck to get that little bitty place over by the pier mirror, Nadine flung open the front door, preparing to call "Miss Ellen!" out into the night. But the night was full of other sounds. Just the ones she was afraid she might get. It was Mr. Frank and all of them shouting and fussing out there in the garage, fit to wake the dead. They were still trying to keep him from going. All at once the noise of Miss Peenie's Thunderbird drowned them out, and Nadine, not waiting to see who it contained as it streaked by, went hurriedly back to the telephone and snatched it up. "Miss Ellen's done gone to the meetin'," she cried, and when the operator told her then that the call was canceled, Nadine slammed down the receiver without a trace of regret. "This is no time for talking to New York City!" she rebuked the instrument and joined Buck at the front door where he listened to the carryings-on beyond.

"—I tell you leave go them fucking car keys—"

"Oh, Lord, Lord," murmured Nadine, shaking her head, and

she closed the door. Buck pried it open.

"—Ye shall not stand in the paths of the righteous! Whores, whoresons! Yea, verily I say unto you—"

Nadine slammed the door good this time. "What you want to hear that filth for?" she upbraided her husband.

"I hope he don't go," Buck said. "He'll wrap hisself around a telephone pole if they let him drive."

Nadine's contempt for his concern at their employer's corporeal being was summed up in a low hissing noise. "You get yourself dressed," she said. "We's goin' to that meetin'. Miss Leta might need us."

She took off for the kitchen, leaving Buck to stow away his cleaning implements and follow. He had no desire to do so, but he knew he would anyway.

A few minutes later, he heard Mr. Frank's Cadillac pull out and he knew they were gone. And maybe Nadine was right: maybe they belonged there tonight, to do what they could to help. Anyway, colored folks were always welcome in the tabernacle, provided they stood discreetly in the back.

It was not the first New Year's Eve Buck had attended, but he was sure it would be like no other. In their correct black on black, he and Nadine set out. Silently, as they drew near the place, they noticed the turn-out for the event. It was always a big show, for Frank Potts conducted his year's-end spiritual harvest as if it were a boxing match staged between Good and Evil. Cars were parked all along the side of the road, and a long line of them cruised slowly along, the drivers alert for a place to stop. People who normally would not be caught dead in the place each year broke off their revels, postponed until later the New Year's toast and ceremonial kissing, or stayed up late just that night, or remained in town an extra day though duty and excitement beckoned elsewhere, all for Frank Potts' New Year's Powerhouse. The admission was free, of course, but the collection plates were passed at the drop of a prayer and the Potts boxes were as regularly located throughout the large drafty hall as stations of the cross in a mighty cathedral. And why? Because of what the town humorists referred to as "the roll call"— that part of the service wherein Brother Potts singled out individuals in special need of repentance, naming names, giving time, place and date. In a town of 7,000 souls, this left little to their fertile imaginations, but with wide grins and much snickering they made do with the small parcel remaining. The next day the victims— great and small—started the new year in blind fury, and as famous as murderers.

Nadine and Buck stood by the entrance, waiting for a break in the pushing, crushing white crowd, and adroitly, seeing their chance, got in. The meeting, to which they had walked, was well under way. The aisles even were jammed, and people were standing in their seats, so as not to miss anything. The news could not have traveled so fast about Frank Potts' defection, so it must be something else. Nadine, on tiptoes, jumped up several times to see, as agile as a basketball player. "Lordee, Lordee," she breathed. "Look at him."

The crowd suddenly cleared, and Buck got a look. Frank Potts was reeling across the stage, catching on to the podium each time he passed, and yelling, Buck realized unmistakably, not something that sounded like, "God damn you, you frigging sinners!" but exactly that.

"Lordee, Lordee," he mourned, hearing it, and bowed his head.

About that time Brother somebody got up and offered a prayer and Brother Potts sank in an attitude of thoughtful repose that could have been achieved only through accident into the thronelike chair behind the podium. Then a Sister somebody else—not quality folks—got up to sing a hymn. Her voice was thin and measly and the hymn endless. People began to sit down once more in their seats to wait it out. But at the fifth verse there spread through the audience a communal sound of awe. Quickly Buck saw his master had stumbled to his feet (apparently Mr. Frank had been sleeping) and was now out in front, standing beside the surprised vocalist, clapping his hands. "Sing out loud and clear, Sister!" roared Brother Potts. "Pick it up! Give it life. God loves Life! You hear, all you sinners?" And as the pianist increased the tempo, Frank Potts not only continued his lusty clapping, but went into a frenzied dance, his large feet sensuously trailing around under his undulating body. The dance was bumps, grinds, rock 'n' roll and the Hula Hoop assembled in an unbelievable medley. And as his clapping continued, the contagion caught hold. The prim soprano shook her skinny hips; people stomped on the floor, the pianist played as if in a trance, or doped. The hymn, now totally travestied, went on and on. People in the audience, transported, joined in, singing in the "unknown tongue." The clapping noise was deafening. And as suddenly as it started it stopped. Frank Potts, seemingly himself again, held up a clay-red huge hand for silence. He got it.

With a certain dignity he went behind the podium, the absolutely silent crowd following every move he made. And he began to preach. "I ain't never heard nothing like it," Nadine murmured a few moments later.

It made her blood quiver, stop, run hot and cold and go on again. He talked about Fire and Ice. He talked about Love like a red-hot flame, and Hell like the ice of Death. He talked about Angels and their searing swords who punctured the sleep and rest of the wicked. He talked about Love Eternal flowing like blood from a cup. He talked about Taking the Lord's Name in Vain; he told of someone who had been struck dead, leaving forever his image in the window glass, visible for all to see when the thunder and its lightning came to whiten the sky. He asked God to strike him dead if he didn't Believe. He asked God to strike him dead if he loved money more than God and extended a dollar bill in his hand and waited—they all waited—for God to strike him dead. Then he bumped his head on the podium and said he was sick with the Frailty of Mankind.

Then the fun began: the roll call. "In these modern, evil times," he intoned, swaying a little, "I have a tale to tell—a modern tale—of sacrifice. Of a father—a just man—as godly and righteous as that old king Shakespeare told about—a feller named Lear— naw, not what you're thinking—he didn't lust, he didn't carnally desire, this man, he *loved*. LOVED!" he thundered. "And who did he love? He loved them daughters who betrayed him—"

"Mercy, Lord," Nadine muttered to herself. "He's after them girls of his."

Buck nudged her. "Miss Ellen's going," he whispered.

Nadine looked. "Thank the dear Lord," she returned and watched along with her husband as Ellen, Mr. Charlesworth holding her arm, disappeared out the side door. No one else seemed to have noticed. With rapt attention, they listened as Brother Potts went on.

XXV

His arm about her shoulders, supporting her, Walter and Ellen looked like two grief-stricken relatives leaving the cemetery as they walked across the parking area marked "For Board Members Only." He helped her into his father's car, a 1937 Buick, the most recent model his eccentric father, who still drove an Electric himself, would tolerate. Then he went around to the other side of the perfectly polished and preserved antique and got in himself. He looked at Ellen, a long doleful gaze, and took her hand. Then he released it and started the engine, as solemnly as if it were a hearse. Leta had requested that he take Ellen home, or to use her exact words: "Get Ellen T.T. out of here. She's going to faint"

Which was not true, but Ellen had allowed herself to be removed, having seen a great deal more than enough. In the crush somehow she and her mother had gotten separated from the others and had ended up seated with Walter; Courtney, if she had come to the services, was elsewhere.

Walter's concern for Ellen was implicit in the way he drove, and now and again he studied her face for symptoms of her condition, as if he were checking her temperature. He said nothing and she knew he was waiting for her to feel strong enough to speak. She had felt strong enough all along, but there seemed to be absolutely nothing to say. What comment could be made? I enjoyed the service; I wish Daddy had drunk hemlock instead of brandy; my witty sister is soon going back to college unless they transfer her to the insane asylum.

They accomplished the drive without a word, and when Walter

pulled into the long driveway, the headlamps briefly bleaching the avenue of trees, Ellen suddenly felt like going anywhere in the world except home. The car swept around the circular part of the drive and came to a stop by the entrance. He turned off the ignition and followed Ellen's gaze which was upward, past the ivy thickly blanketing the old brick walls, to her room on the second floor in the west wing of the sprawling gingerbread monstrosity that was home. How I hate that room, was what she was thinking, but she said, "I see I left my lights on."

Walter smiled at this, grateful to be smiling again. But he could think of nothing light to say; no appropriate banter came to uncramp his mind.

Ellen sighed heavily. "Well, if I must, I must," she said regretfully, still looking toward the house.

"Want me to come in for a while?" he asked.

Her smile was wan. "I don't know why two New Year's eves should be spoiled."

He grinned at this. "You mean we each have a separate one?" he asked, delighted at the opportunity to joke. "I thought there was just a single that had to do for everybody."

She laughed. "Walter, I really don't want to go in," she told him.

"Good heavens, child, why didn't you say so?" he asked in relieved astonishment. "Want to go someplace for a drink?"

"Yes," she said smiling. "New York."

"Excellent choice," he replied and immediately started the car. "And we'll just stop off on the way and have a little liquid nourishment. How about if your old cuz bought you some bubbly and toasted your health?"

The prospect seemed to bring Ellen back to life. She sat up alertly, rolled down her window as they drove along and took a couple of deep breaths. "Um, good," she commented, then asked,

"What glamorous night spot are you taking me to?" she asked.

"I'll give you your choice," he said. "There's the Brown Jug and then there's always the Brown Jug."

Ellen laughed. "I guess it would be better to go to the Brown Jug." It was the only place in town that would be open this late, but she wondered if Walter seriously thought they would be able to get champagne there. After all, it was only a roadhouse and naturally the specialty was beer. She considered reminding Walter of this, but maybe he had just meant champagne figuratively. If so, she thought rather wistfully, beer would just have to do. Anything available would have to do, for tonight she wanted a drink.

But Walter had meant champagne, and solved the problem neatly. They first drove out to her great uncle Will's house and Ellen, waiting in the car while Walter sneaked inside, felt as daring as he did, though it was all rather silly. When Walter came back, triumphantly holding up the two quart bottles of champagne cadged from his father's supply, Ellen giggled in delight.

"It isn't chilled, alas," Walter whispered as he came back to the car. "But I reckon they'll put it in the freezer for us and it won't take too long." He got inside, nimble as a schoolboy, a prankish look on his face. There in the near darkness Ellen could almost believe he was her own age, and for the first time saw how he must have looked when he was young.

The spirit of the lark continued as they drove the few miles to the Little Brown Jug, as it was properly called, parked the car, and sailed inside, their cheeks fresh, their eyes bright.

The owner assured them the champagne would be ready in no time and meantime served them icy bottles of beer accompanied by two frosted tumblers. It being only just after midnight, the road-house was still deserted except for two other couples seated in a booth across the barnlike room, and the presence of Ellen and Walter was very welcome. Ellen and Walter, seated opposite each other in their booth, grinned in camaraderie and drank their beer. They made faces of disgust when the jukebox started up with a loud, twanging rock 'n' roll tune, but watched fascinated as the other two couples danced, going through their gyrations with earnest, vacant faces and consummate skill; they took their rock 'n' roll very seriously.

"Why don't you teach me to do that, Cuz," Walter said playfully, and Ellen informed him that he knew as much about that teenage art as she did.

"Where did you get all your high fallutin' ideas?" he asked. "Now Leta, when she was your age was doing the Big Apple and Swing and everything just like any other popular gal in town. She didn't sit home with her nose—"

"In a book," Ellen supplied, and added that she didn't have any high fallutin' ideas, whatever that meant; that she had always just wanted one thing: to be an actress.

Walter shook his head; she was just beyond him. He didn't understand where people got such aspirations from, especially if they were born and reared in little country towns. Ellen reminded him that was where most actresses came from and said that now was as good time as any to tell him, at least, that she had every intention of going back to New York—at once.

Walter looked embarrassed. "I don't know how to say this, Cuz, but your Daddy phoned up Cousin Ella and told her to tell Sissy to say you wouldn't be rejoining the cast."

The bastard, thought Ellen. "What else has he done, Walter, or would you rather not say?" she asked acidly.

"He asked me and Courtney a whole lot about you," he admitted.

"And you told him exactly what?"

"We were all just trying to help you, honey."

"In what way?" Ellen inquired.

"So we could catch that McCoy fellow and put him behind bars where he belongs."

"And did you?" Ellen asked; stunned to hear Stephen's name on her cousin's lips.

"No. It seems your friend Gloria or somebody gave him some money so he could skip town."

"How do you know all this?"

"I had my office hire a private detective. They just telephoned me this afternoon."

"*You* hired a private detective? Why you?"

Walter shrugged. "It was your Daddy's idea. He knew our firm often has occasion to hire detectives and he felt they would know who was reliable, so I telephoned them to get somebody on this business."

So that was why Walter and Courtney had been asked to dinner tonight, Ellen thought. So Walter could give his report. It was also why her father had asked that she join them. Sadistically, he had planned to have her present to be confronted with her guilt. "How many days did it take the Pinkerton agents to unearth all this?"

"They've been on it about four days."

"And did Daddy commend you on your excellent work, and did you get a chance tonight to tell him the extent of your success?"

"Now, look here, Ellen. We are all just trying to protect you. The only clue I gave was that you had once mentioned to me that a young fellow had followed you from Chicago—"

"—And I suppose you discovered it was just the other way around?"

Walter nodded gravely. "We got a pretty thorough report, Ellen. But a whole lot of it I knew already—a lot of things I didn't tell your Daddy when he asked—"

"Why not?" she asked bitingly.

"'Because,'" he said, "I'm very fond of you."

"But not too fond not to help him meddle in my life and do a little private meddling on your own…"

"I didn't think of it that way. You are a minor—"

"Did you know Steve's name before?"

"Yes," he said. "But I didn't connect him with what happened to you. You see, Courtney and I believed you when you said the person was a stranger."

Ellen gave a nasty laugh. "Point one for me."

"Ellen, you've nearly been in very grave trouble." "Thank you for the information."

"Do you realize it could ruin you for life? and ruin your whole family? If this got out, why, your daddy's career—"

Ellen's sharp peal of laughter rang so loudly that the other occupants turned to stare. "Daddy's just ruined his own career!" she reminded Walter. "And I suppose he'll blame that on me too. No wonder he started his roll call with me and Peenie! I'm sure he'll air every sordid detail your detectives dug up just to prove to himself and the whole of Crump, North Carolina just what a long-suffering saintly man he is!"

"I didn't get an opportunity to tell him very much," Walter said.

"No?" said Ellen in icy fury. "Here. Here's a dime. Why don't you go phone him at the tabernacle. Then he can go back to his audience and really give them a sermon."

"If I were you," said Walter. "I'd just sit still a minute and listen. What I was going to say was that I hadn't made up my mind, whether I'd had the chance to tell him or not, just how much to tell him. I had wanted to talk to you first."

"When did you plan to do that?" Ellen asked searingly. "At the supper table? You certainly haven't made a move in my direction. Why don't you just tell me, Walter, precisely what your detectives told you and what you found out on your own—not that I'll ever believe a word you say again."

"I haven't lied to you, little girl. I was simply trying to look out for you since you didn't seem to know how to look out for yourself. After all, you come from a very prominent and wealthy family—"

"Come on, Walter," she cut in. "Just give me the facts."

And at that minute the champagne arrived. The owner himself brought it, beaming with festive pleasure. Walter bopped up and insisted on opening it himself, responding with amazing ease to the change of pace. He also insisted that the owner join them in one glass at least, and the owner hurried away for another frosted tumbler—the only glasses, he apologized, that they had in the house.

"Just pour mine right in here," Ellen instructed Walter, her voice tight and mean.

"Right on top of the beer?"

"Yes."

Walter said he wouldn't dream of it.

"Then I don't want any," Ellen said, and with an ugly gesture pushed her glass aside.

Walter placed it in front of her and poured, fully conscious that it was not the champagne she was defiling so much as his gift.

Ellen gulped it down, not bothering to wait for their guest, and extended the glass for more. Walter filled it, and this she drank off without a glance toward him or the proprietor who had rejoined them and was graciously toasting her health.

Once the man had gone, she said, "Okay, canary. Sing."

As Walter talked, his voice starched with anger, his words precise and crisp as an Englishman's, Ellen helped herself continually from the champagne bottle. Once she picked up Walter's discarded beer by mistake, but drank it anyway. It simply did not matter.

She listened to all he had to say, not troubling to interrupt with denials or corroborations. The champagne was beginning to affect her, and her look lost its intensity and became dreamy, as did her temper. Somewhere in the middle of his discourse she found herself feeling positively tender toward him for all the trouble he had gone to for her sake, and moreover, an odd relief that there was seemingly nothing to hide. She felt herself smiling at him.

He noticed it at once, and his expression lost some of its anxiety. "Are you beginning to forgive me?" he broke off his recital to ask.

She nodded, but said nothing, so he went on. He told her that his real suspicions and worry had been aroused that night they had had a nightcap together in the Barbizon Plaza; all of it had been so strange—the unpleasant encounter with that man with the familiar manner; her obviously upset reaction; her confession that she had been in New York for quite some time. After that he had made some inquiries—he didn't say where or what—and had learned the name of the young man from Chicago, and just what kind of a fellow he was. Then he had privately enlisted the aid of Mr. Logan Harper who, being informed of the situation, understood perfectly and proved most cooperative. Through his friend Sam, the toilet-seat magnate and a well-known theatrical angel, Mr. Harper found out a little about Gloria. Walter did not say so, but Ellen surmised that Sam had discreetly pumped Victor Rose. More about Stephen came to light—namely, his propensity for living off of women— as well as Gloria's past, vastly cleaned up, Ellen noted with satisfaction, for Walter only indicated that the girl had lived a fairly rough life. Just how rough and to what extent Ellen and Stephen had been involved in it Walter had not known until the detectives informed him. And while the accuracy of their detail was startling in some instances, there were thankfully great lacunae in the complete account; there was no inference, for example, of their swindling or shoplifting, but there was much inference that Stephen was a pimp and Ellen and Gloria had been his whores for some months until each, in his and her own way, had landed on more solid ground.

Walter finally stopped, his message at an end. He looked at Ellen's dreamy face and waited for her to make a comment. He then saw that she was pretty drunk. "You can see what an earthquake all this would have caused if I'd told your daddy," he said.

She nodded. "I suppose the only thing left is suicide," she said thickly, so startling Walter that he thought she was serious until he saw a sarcastic little smile on her lips.

"I don't know what to make of you, Ellen Tate Terrill."

"Make nothing," she said coldly. "But get this through your head, dear cousin: I am not a whore."

He looked at her doubtfully. "It's not my business."

"Oh, yes it is," she sprang to life. "You've made it your business."

"If I have interfered," he said, "it was only out of love."

Ellen laughed at him, throwing back her head dramatically. "I'm enjoying myself," she said. "Give me some more champagne."

"There's not any more."

"Beer, then. Anything."

"You've had enough."

"But you haven't, dear cousin. I want you to get good and tight."

"Why?" he asked and there was an undercurrent of interest in his voice.

"You'll see," she said.

He got up, excusing himself and went to confer with the owner of the Brown Jug. She watched them talking together, and in a few minutes Walter came back to the table with a pint of whisky. "He's bringing the branch water," he said in obvious good humor.

She watched every motion he made, her eyes following his hands as he poured whisky into the tumblers, measuring it out too liberally, and she knew drunkenly that she had been wrong: he, too, was feeling no pain. Without waiting for his precious branch water, he tossed off his whisky neat. She did the same. "Let's dance," she said and was already on the floor before he had replied.

Arms about each other's waists, they strolled toward the jukebox to select a number. Ellen vaguely noticed that the place was filling up; soon it would be crowded. People were staring at them and she reflected that she was now a sort of old curiosity shop, for these starers must have just come from her father's portals.

The music began and sinuously Ellen pressed herself against her cousin. She was determined to play this thing for all it was worth. "You like to dance, don't you, Walter?" she breathed at him.

"Yes," he said.

"With me?"

"With you,"

That, she decided, was enough for now, and after the music stopped, she went back to their booth. The dance had evidently increased Walter's thirst, for he poured another liberal helping of whisky for himself and for her. He had a little trouble in getting the pitcher of water accurately aimed at their glasses. Ellen smiled genially at all this, and watched him as he drank. "Are you in love with Courtney, Walter?" she asked.

A troubled cloud of a look passed over his face. He suggested that they dance. Ellen inclined her head in agreement, her smile amused.

Again she held herself close to him, deliberately clinging, and felt his body respond. He cupped his hand around her head caressingly, but said nothing. She knew it wasn't yet time for her to speak.

Then they went back to their booth, and after another drink, he opened up and poured out his marital misery to her. But as yet he had not said what Ellen waited for: that he was crazy about Ellen; would give anything to have her. Only the anticipation of this kept her sober enough to go on drinking, drink for drink with him. They danced quite a lot in between, each visit to the dance floor increasing, she knew, Walter's desire.

When Walter's declaration finally came, Ellen, having expected it so long, was unprepared. He was holding her hand as they sat together side by side in the booth, and his preamble to it was mostly in looks of ardor. "I'm madly in love with you," he mumbled. "Wrong though it may be."

All she was really sure she heard was the "wrong though it may be." But before she had a chance to assimilate this he had gone on, and the rudeness of what he said shocked her. "You can't know what this means to me, Ellen. Please," he kissed her fingers. "Please be nice to me. You know what I mean—like you were to the others."

"What others?" she asked.

"The other men."

"Suppose I told you there weren't any?"

But he wasn't listening.

"—I'll do anything, anything."

"Divorce Courtney?"

"I'll give you money, keep you—"

"You make me sick," she said. At last she had been given the perfect moment to say it.

"—if you'll just be nice to me," he muttered on, still at her fingers.

"Sleep with you, you mean?"

"Darling!" he said in an ecstasy.

"Suppose I say no," she asked. "What then?"

"You can't hurt me this way, you wouldn't——"

"Wouldn't I?"

He tried to take her face between his hands, giving her a drunken gaze of love. "You wouldn't want to hurt me any more than I want to hurt you——"

"I want to kill you, that's all!" she said between clenched teeth.

"No, Ellen, no. You don't want to hurt your daddy this way—don't make me do it——"

She wrenched herself away and got to her feet.

As far as she knew, he was still back there in the booth as she drove Uncle Will's car away, sobbing the bitter tears of the drunken frustrated lover.

XXVI

There was quite a crowd around her, and though she had felt several prodding her with a foot she still continued to play dead, hoping that somehow they would lose interest and go away. But they didn't. They milled about murmuring, conjecturing. Someone remarked that she looked just asleep or passed out; someone else commented on the fact that she was pretty young to be in this condition, but here in the Village you never knew about these beatniks. It wasn't until she caught the word "Bellevue" that she sprang to her feet, and sprinted off around the corner of Bank Street and Waverly, as agile as a track star, running like she had not run since physical education class at Sweet Briar. When she came to number twenty, Bank Street, she galloped up the stoop, threw open the door and galloped up the stairs, back to the party.

"Hello, everybody," she panted as she rushed in.

"Oh, hello, Pottsy. You been up to your usual tricks?" asked the host. He, Grant King Ledbetter, one of Apple Ashby's dearest friends was a most elegant young man and he certainly, most definitely did not approve of Apple's alliance, even though it was substantially over in that part, with a girl like Pottsy. Look at the way she dressed, just for instance, the same old blue jeans month after month, and that horrid smelly sweater. You'd think she could at least wash that hair of hers once in a while—or cut it. He took it as an insult that Apple had insisted on bringing the "poor thing" into his house, even if there were going to be lots of people. Coolly, he turned from this offensive creature, presenting his broad squat

197

back to her, in its beautifully tailored madras jacket, setting his ankles in their long socks above the new and expensive Bermuda socks in a pose of firm defiance, and spoke to a sympathetic guest.

"What do you mean, 'up to my usual tricks'?" she asked belligerently, putting a hand on his shoulder to turn him around. They were about the same height, and though his weight and breadth promised power, she could outdo him in a prize fight any day. She had smacked him across the face once in Apple's bookshop, and had given him a terrific shove that sent him crashing through the first editions case. That was really what bugged him.

"Oh, go turn on somewhere," he said tiredly over his shoulder and brushed off her hand. He expected the chain of vituperative obscenity this got him, and he ignored it too. But he could feel her there behind him. She was still asking what he had meant by his crack about tricks. "If there's anything I can't stand it's a paranoid bull dyke," he remarked to his friend and then turned to Pottsy. "Look, dear, why don't you go off to somebody else's party? I told you—Apple told you before you came—that there wouldn't be any pot—just martinis. If you can't behave yourself, just this once, I think you'd better leave. You're embarrassing me and my guests."

Ellen looked around the chic but minute living room; the guests all appeared to be so clean. So nice. Tears welled up and coursed down her cheeks. "I told you martinis make me sleepy!" she sobbed and staggered away, falling across the feet of the guest who sat in Grant's brand-new and much prized Eames chair. "Go to hell!" she muttered by way of apology, and went over to an empty corner to collapse on the floor, a seating arrangement she preferred anywhere.

A new arrival looked at her with interest and asked who she was and what she was talking about. They both listened to her almost incoherent mumbling. "Oh, she's griping about Grant probably, or life, or Affectation, her favorite subject."

"Well, *she* certainly has no right to talk. I never such an outrageous and pathetic disguise in all my life. And she's not bad-looking either. Who does she think she is? Miss Greenwich Village?"

They listened another moment or two: Pottsy was audibly criticizing Grant's "ancient-modern tastes; a good ten years behind the uptown chic faggots."

"What a bore! Who brought her anyway?"

"I did," said Apple. "Pottsy's a fine person. She comes from a very fine family down South."

This brought a hoot of derision from the pair. "I notice you said 'comes,'" one remarked with sarcasm and looked around for appreciation of his wit.

"That, I will never believe," Grant said, overhearing the conversation and joining them. "My family has lived in North Carolina for generations and I can assure you no one in the state ever heard of the Pottses. Potts indeed!" he gave an ugly little laugh of amusement.

"I don't know anything about it," said Apple. "I've never been South."

"Well, *I* know something about it!" Grant took over. "She's some kind of hillbilly or factory worker or something, just trying to crash the Village by pulling out all the stops. Oh, I'm sure she's *sensitive* and *intelligent*, Apple. But, my dear, the creature is not well bred. If she went to Sweet Briar—ever went near it—so did I."

"Entirely possible," someone simpered.

"Now is that nice?" Grant wanted to know. Then, in self-mockery added, "At least I'm a lady," and to the amusement of all minced away, in excellent parody. Grant was famous in a small way for his mummery and wit.

The party, as delicate and refined as a teacup, went on. No one got falling-down drunk; only high and epigrammatical and attractive. At midnight they all left and Apple, staying behind a few minutes to help Grant clear—poor sweet angel had to get up so early with his new job—confided she was so worried about Pottsy. "I'm afraid if she keeps going like this she'll really fall through the bottom. She's been running around with all that crowd on horse."

"I know," said Grant. "I was walking through the Square on Sunday and I saw her making a perfect ass of herself with that guitar player. She was necking with him, right on the fountain. It even embarrassed *me*, of all people, and like Errol Flynn, I've seen everything twice."

"I'm afraid she'll land in Bellevue again. I tried to keep an eye on her tonight, but I suppose she went for her usual 'walk' and fell asleep in the gutter somewhere."

"Does she really have any family, Apple? Here, sweetie, let me get you another drink."

Ellen came to just then, but remained curled up on the floor lazily listening. They were really on the subject of her finances, now, and Apple was feeling sorry for herself.

"She keeps saying she'll inherit a pile of money next year when she's twenty-two—"

"Twenty-two? Why twenty-two? I wouldn't believe a word of it, sweetie. She's just taking you."

"Maybe you're right. Maybe she is just telling me that to cushion the blow."

"How much is she into you for?"

"I wouldn't know. Mostly nickels and dimes and food and things, but these mount up."

"You can't smoke marijuana for free. Of course it's obvious she doesn't spend any money on clothes." He gave a nasty laugh.

"I think she's too proud to take anything except what she needs."

"This brought a roar of laughter from the audience, as they say in books," he remarked.

"I believe if she ever does get any money she'll pay me back."

There was a silence, then Grant spoke again. "Poor sweetie. You have had it bad, haven't you? My God, baby, why can't you straighten out your love life? Now I, for instance, having had the experience you had with that horrid uncouth Steve McCoy would have known better than *ever* to even say 'hy'do' to anyone he'd ever met even—much less one of his great friends who had 'known' him, as they say in the Bible."

"I didn't take her in on Steve's recommendation," Apple reminded him, annoyed. "I didn't even know she knew him when she came around to the shop asking me for a job."

"Well, the minute you found out she did you should have gotten rid of her. Besides, you said she was the worst lover you ever had."

"I didn't, darling. I just said I brought her out and then she decided to go back in again. She really wasn't cut out to be a les."

"You always say that about the ones who don't work out."

"Don't be a bitch. Anyway I'm not so keen on the life myself."

Grant gave a low, snarling laugh. "How many big, sadistic, complete heels like Stephen McCoy do you think there are in this world?" he asked.

"Enough," she said coolly. "Remember I've turned a trick a time or two for you."

"Darling, you know he wasn't my type."

"I never *offered* you Stephen," she said acidly.

"And I never had him, sweetie," he replied airily. "—And didn't have the faintest desire to. You can believe that or not. Anyway, didn't I hear you telling someone he's now carrying on with God?"

Apple laughed appreciatively. "Yes, it's the most fantastic thing. Didn't I tell you? I'm sure I did. You know he writes to me constantly—or did—some guilt feeling I suppose."

"Yes, you told me about the part after he tried to make like a Mexican bullfighter and met this Catholic dame and got all involved with Mother Church—wasn't he a fallen-away Catholic or something to begin with?"

"Yes. Cradle. I told you. Anyway, he wrote me the most *passionate* letters about her. But it seems she was married and completely faithful to husband and God, so he applied the old principle of if you can't beat them, join them. So that's what he's done. The last letter—at least he says it's the last forever—which I got day before yesterday was mailed from Springfield, Kentucky. He's gone down there to join the Trappists."

Grant laughed and made some snide remarks about Thomas Merton and Stephen's always knowing a good thing when he saw it.

"Oh, I don't think he'll break his vows—once he takes them," Apple said. "Stephen was always deeply religious. Everything he did indicated it. He was just a perfectionist and felt covered with sin, so since he couldn't be perfectly wonderful he tried to be perfectly awful."

"He should have settled for that success," Grant commented. "But don't you think it's peculiar, sweetie, for him to write all this to you?"

Apple considered this. "No," she said. "Stephen loved me enormously in his way. And l think he loved Ellen—"

"Who? Oh, Ellen! That was a stroke of genius of mine, wasn't it, nicknaming her Pottsy—"

"It never really fit her," Apple said. "She's neither a patsy nor a hophead."

"—Good facsimile."

"I've got to go."

"I'd beg you to stay, baby. But I must get off to beddy-bye if ever I'm going to be starry-eyed and bushy-tailed for Madison Avenue tomorrow."

"Help me wake up Pottsy. No, don't smack her cheeks. You know that makes her furious."

"It's the best way I know to rouse the unconscious. Oh, you little faker, you! Look, sweetie, she's been awake all this time."

"*Ne touche pas*, you lousy fag," said Ellen and glowered at him from the floor. She only consented to rise when Apple extended her hand.

## XXVII

Listlessly, Ellen sat in the corner of Apple's bookshop while Apple, busy at the desk reading *The Antiquarian Bookman* and checking off items she had in stock called for in their "Books Wanted" section, pretended she wasn't there. They had just opened the shop for the day and had just had another quarrel of a multiple compounded nature. Apple couldn't remember all of the ingredients that had gone into it, but foremost among those she could was Ellen's continued inertia which prevented her from lifting a hand in here: for instance, Apple had asked her to wash down the shelves in the drama section and Ellen had said she couldn't bear to touch anything connected with the subject. This was going *too* far; so her theatrical career was a fizzle. What had that to do with washing shelves? Apple was sensitive too, but not completely crazy. Then they had started on Gratitude and how Ellen had no drive; she could call up that cousin of hers in that new show if she wanted to. What made Ellen think the girl hated her? There was some deep, dark and probably silly secret Ellen had buried which all had to do with her last visit home—well over a year ago, which was before Apple had met her. All Ellen had ever said was that she had left for good, had suddenly decamped on New Year's Eve, had driven to Charlotte and hopped the first plane out without a good-bye to anybody. Had she heard from her family since? No. And as far as Apple knew they had not tried to get in touch with her. But of course Ellen was so secretive—

But at least Ellen wasn't threatening suicide today, nor had she turned on, though Apple knew Ellen still had several sticks. Wearily, she put down *The Antiquarian Bookman* and picked up *Publishers' Weekly*, the other "must" in the way of trade literature. They were still running ads, she saw, for that new book: MANY ARE CALLED. What a title. If she were going to write a book about her life as a prostitute, provided she had had such a life, she would certainly have chosen a better title. But it was selling like mad. Of course Apple wouldn't stock such trash, even if the subject were all the rage. Her customers didn't need that kind of literary titillation; if they wanted pornography there were better things. She observed with a degree of satisfaction that it had at least fallen to third place on the Bestseller List. But this would set up the publishers of MANY ARE CALLED for life; they'd never had such a success. That was the way small houses, however, got to be big ones. Idly she read the ad and looked at the picture of this frank, daring authoress. Pretty enough to be a model; maybe t.b. had slimmed her down. That's why she had written it—in two weeks—from a t.b. sanitorium when she thought she was going to die. And when she didn't, "she had had the courage," so read the blurb, "to publish the book, under her own name, in the hope that her story would help others and give them the same will for living a rich, useful life that she had found—" Bosh, Apple thought. "Shit! Junk!" she said aloud and angrily turned the page. Ellen vaguely looked up, but then looked down again, lost in her neurosis.

"Why don't you try to get a job modeling, Pottsy?" Apple idly called.

Pottsy did not bother to answer her, and Apple went on reading. Again she was confronted with news about MANY ARE CALLED. Why, why, would anybody publish a book under that title? It sounded like a handbook for Presbyterian ministers. Only amateurs would think it could sell—which just went to show. "Good God!" she exclaimed aloud. "Listen to this, Pottsy," but a glance in Pottsy's direction assured Apple that she wouldn't, so she read on silently to herself. The biggest price for the movie rights since FOREVER AMBER. Oh, well. She yawned. "Lunchtime, Pottsy," she called. "Shall I close the shop and we both go, or will you watch it?"

"I'll watch it," Ellen said. "I'm not hungry."

"You're sure you'll really *watch* it now?" Apple questioned her. "And not go to sleep with your head on the desk."

"I'll watch it, Apple," Ellen promised. "I feel okay today. And I'm sorry we quarreled."

"That's what I like about you, kid. You're honest." But all the same she gave several backward looks of misgiving as she left the shop. She was awfully worried about Ellen. She was just slipping away. And the next time Bellevue got her, she'd be sent off to the happy farm.

She turned into the corner drugstore and picked up THE POST and THE MIRROR to read while she ate. She started with THE POST. Last night's, of course, but she never saw it except here. Again that ubiquitous authoress, Gloria Wayne. An excerpt, no less, and an interview. Apple ordered a chicken liver sandwich and read while she waited for it. Avidly she soaked up the details offered about Miss Wayne's "heroic struggles." She was back in New York, living quietly on the East Side, and writing another book. "She is intelligent, beautiful, modest and well read," said the interviewer's description—what a combination of goodies! Apple commented to herself and read on. "Planning to be married soon to a man she knew before she contracted t.b....faithfully loyal throughout her illness—" (Faithfully loyal! Stephen would have liked that sentence) "Will give proceeds of movie rights to sanitarium...." Apple broke off. It was too much. These gushy fools, and imagine comparing such a creature's style and mind to Gypsy Rose Lee! She picked up half of her sandwich and began to read the excerpt, apparently from the middle of the book. "—When I first met Ellen P., I had never seen or dreamed of meeting anyone quite like her. She was as frail as a feather, with hair almost as light, and blue faded eyes that looked out at one like the wisdom of the sky—" My God, thought Apple. The wisdom of the sky. The space age is really here. But she continued to read. "…She came from some small Southern town, of a prominent and rich family and she did not need to live as the three of us lived. I never understood her, but I admired her, for she remained principled just as we remained unprincipled. I think it was only through Ellen that we, S. and I, found the sky. One day I hope to tell her all that she—"

Apple put the paper down and also her sandwich. This was Gloria Wayne; the Gloria Wayne of the Stephen Gloria Wayne. And Ellen P. was, of course—

She scrambled off the stool, catching the heel of her sandal so that the strap broke. Hurriedly, she yanked it from her foot and went out the door like a cyclone, one shoe off, one shoe on, and tore back to the shop. Thank God Ellen was still here, and not asleep. Instead she was talking quietly to a Helen Hokinson type, explaining that this was not a rental library.

Apple, breathless, waited, restoring her broken shoe surreptitiously to her foot. Yes, Ellen's eyes were like that poor thing. Did that Gloria really mean it about wanting to tell her, or was it just something in the book?

She went to the telephone. Would such a person have a listed number? Why not? She dialed Information and asked for a new listing for a Miss Gloria Wayne up on the East Side somewhere. The operator at once supplied the number. Apple dialed it.

"Hello?" the voice was gentle and subdued, "modest," just as THE POST had said.

"Hello, this is Apple Ashby. Are you the same Gloria Wayne?"

"Yes, hello Apple."

"I've been reading about you. And I wondered—do you really want to find Ellen Potts—and help her?"

"More than anything."

"Just a minute," Apple said, and called, "Pottsy, here's somebody who wants to speak to you."